THE CHRISTMAS EVE MURDERS

David J. Kinsella

THE
CHRISTMAS EVE
MURDERS

To Patricia, the brightest star in my universe.

PROLOGUE

Unseen hands propel him relentlessly forward through deep snowdrifts.

From one side of his ragged blindfold, he catches a fleeting glimpse of shadowy trees, their branches weighed down heavily by snow. Each labored breath burns cold in his lungs. *Fight!* Responding to his mind's urgent command, he tests the bindings for what seems like the hundredth time since this waking nightmare began. Despite his struggle, his wrists remain firmly tied behind him, cut painfully by biting cords of rope. He flexes his fingers in an attempt to restore some measure of feeling in his hands, but they remain stubbornly numb. Losing balance, he pitches forward, and his face makes sudden impact with the frozen ground.

For a moment, he lies still. The quietness broken only by his heartbeat hammering loudly in his ears. A welcome respite. The invigorating scent of pine trees. *Do something!* His conscience urges him on again, yet fatigue drags him down into the comfort of the darkness, embracing him in its icy caress. He sinks deeper and deeper, his mind desperately seeking any avenue of escape from the horror that has befallen him. *Please let this be over.*

The silence is shattered by the stuttering sound of an engine starting up, saturating the air with the unmistakable heady smell of diesel. Somewhere nearby, there is a gentle flutter as a flock of birds take flight in alarm. Loud machinery grinds and grates, its screeching magnified in the heavy stillness of the winter's night. Without warning, his captor pulls him unceremoniously to his feet and shoves him onto a bed of cold moving metal. *Fight, you idiot!* But his body fails to respond. Utter exhaustion consumes him. He has a detached sensation that he is watching the scene unfold from above, as though his spirit has finally conceded that this is not a fight he can win.

How did I end up here? A prickling feeling of freezing rain on his skin signals to him that the end is near. His body trembles from shock and the onset of hypothermia.

What are the chances of something like this happening to me?

He screams silently into his gag, tears rolling down his face. Heavy ropes encircle his waist and shoulders, pinning him to the platform, like a sacrificial lamb being prepared for slaughter.

The discordant symphony of mechanical gears in full operation is deafening. No precious moments of his life appear before his eyes. Nothing affords him any recap of the last thirty-odd years of his banal existence. His blindfold mercifully slips again to provide him one final parting gift; a view of the heavens, its endless expanse of deep blue scattered with the constellations. A line of a poem he learned at high school surfaces in his mind, offering a comforting hand as he slides away into the abyss. The soothing lullaby ripples through his thoughts. *And I have miles to go before I sleep.*

The darkness explodes into splinters of blinding light.

Somewhere distant, church bells chime. It will be Christmas soon.

PART I – THE CITY

"I intend, sir, to make of this the finest police force in the world."

—George Washington Matsell, First New York City Police Commissioner, July 1874.

CHAPTER 1

The Case File

Detective Ryan's desk was littered with papers. To the untrained eye, they were scattered about without any apparent order. Ryan knew better. He was assembling the patchwork of facts in front of him to bring structure and meaning to the chaos, to cast light on the malicious deeds that whispered and mocked him from the shadows.

He drained the last mouthful of coffee and crumpled the paper cup, tossing it into the nearby trash can. The office of the New York Police Department's twentieth precinct was a hive of activity. The air hummed with energy. It was 8 a.m., and last night in Manhattan had brought with it a new wave of crimes and cases to be investigated and resolved. He sighed as he glanced at the towering bundle of incident reports in front of him. Just another day at the office.

Detective work was like panning for gold. You had to filter away all the debris, all the useless dirt that distracted you and end up with the truth. The motivation behind the wrongdoing usually led like a trail of breadcrumbs to the human frailties that were the ultimate catalyst for the crime.

Ryan specialized in cases that no one else could solve or, indeed, wanted to solve. The ones that had no leads or culminated in a tangle of dead ends that seemed to go nowhere. He had carved out a reputation of being the detective who got things done. He glanced out of the nearby window to the city below. The sky was leaden with clouds and snowflakes performed a hypnotic dance in all directions. Millions of people. Millions of interactions. It was a war of emotions out there, the battlefield strewn with countless victims. Some God-fearing folk kept their desires in check, while others gave in to the whispers of anger, envy, and revenge that spurred them on to commit offenses most would learn to regret. Woven through this tapestry of sorrow were the crimes of the deranged that had no basis in motivation, other than the victim simply being at the wrong place, at the wrong time.

He rubbed the dark stubble on his chin pensively as he looked at the case file in front of him. His scribbled notes from last night were somewhat cryptic to him now, as though he had experienced a moment of delirium while writing them. He stared at the date on the corner of his latest entry he had made earlier today; "December 24."

In an effort to aid his memory on each file, he had long ago abandoned relying on case file numbers, which were eventually used to archive all of the documents. Somehow a number alone just didn't feel right for a collection of paperwork that was the source of so much pain. Instead, he allocated a specific name to each of his files. All the victims were real people. He felt they deserved more than just a file number to mark their passing.

He closed the file. "The Christmas Eve Murders" was written in his tidy handwriting across the front cover. It seemed almost hypocritical. *Who associated Christmas with murder anyway?* He chuckled cynically to himself at that thought. That was civilian thinking. He knew a different world, where Christmas represented a time where old wounds re-opened and where the pictures on the television of happy homes and festive cheer only fueled the fires of loneliness and despair that threatened to engulf others. He stared, lost in thought, at the sad looking red and silver garlands that adorned the ceiling of the office, offering a rather feeble attempt at Christmas cheer.

His reverie was broken by footsteps beside his desk and someone clearing their throat. Ryan turned around in his swivel chair to see his newly assigned cadet, standing with a pile of papers clutched to his chest. He cleared his throat again nervously.

Ryan saved him the embarrassment and broke the awkward silence. "Morning, Tony. How you doing?"

The cadet tugged anxiously on his tie, which appeared to be in the process of throttling him. "Yeah, good, boss. Good."

"You read those papers I gave you?" the detective asked, gesturing casually to the dog-eared pile of documents Tony was holding tightly.

"Yup. Interesting, boss. Very . . . interesting."

Ryan arched an eyebrow. "Interesting? They weren't supposed to be interesting. You were supposed to learn something from that file. Evidence gathering. Building the case. Stuff like that."

Tony gave a feeble nod.

The detective leaned back in his chair, clasping his hands behind his head. "So, summarize the case file for me. What do you think? Any connections? Similar modus operandi?"

The cadet gave him a startled look for a moment before gathering his thoughts. "Six homicides," he said slowly, as he recalled the details of the file. "Over six years. One murder, each year, on Christmas Eve."

Ryan grunted in approval. "And what day is it today, Tony?"

The cadet considered this for a moment, expecting a trick question, which the detective liked to pull on him every so often to keep him on his toes. "Yeah. Christmas Eve."

There was an awkward silence. Ryan didn't want the kid to have a heart attack in his first week, so he moved his hand in a charitable, circular gesture, indicating that the cadet likely had more thoughts to offer up on the case.

Tony swallowed hard. "All victims had a . . . Just a second." He leafed clumsily through the file and paused purposefully at a page as he searched the text. "A small arrow-like bruising on their heads."

Ryan nodded, waiting for the young detective to provide further insights. However, the cadet was released from his uncomfortable confrontation by the sound of high heels clipping on the floor as Lizzy, the office administrator, floated by in a cloud of perfume. She held a sprig of mistletoe in her outstretched hand, festooned with small silver bells.

"Morning, Ryan, how about a little peck? Just a little kiss, seeing how it's Christmas and all." She pursed her lips in exaggeration and threw back her blond hair.

The detective looked around for someone to save him, realizing with growing panic that there was no one coming. "You know I would, Lizzy. But my missus might get upset."

She moved closer still, the smell of her perfume intoxicating. "Oh Ryan. I won't tell," she whispered.

Ryan squirmed and ran a hand nervously through his hair, which he always wore tidily slicked back. Lizzy's formal job title was office administrator and receptionist, but her job description appeared to include mocking Ryan whenever the opportunity presented itself, and Ryan had to admit, she was pretty good at it. "I'm married, Lizzy," he offered, hoping that would end the conversation.

She leaned towards him, her long hair gently touching Ryan's shoulder. "Well, that didn't stop Teddy and Steve," she said conspiratorially in a hushed voice.

Ryan reclined back in his chair as far as he could. He teetered precariously on the edge of overbalancing and falling.

Tony stepped forward, brushing one hand through his brown, unruly hair. "Eh, Lizzy. I'm here, you know. Available . . . and all. Just saying."

Lizzy laughed loudly. "Oh now, Tony. Don't be silly. I'd get in trouble for corrupting a minor."

Tony looked positively horrified. "Hey, I'm nineteen! I'm —"

The nearby telephone rang loudly.

Ryan straightened in his chair. His prayers had been answered. Lizzy looked at the phone on her desk, her shoulders slumping as she knew her round of torturing Ryan had come to a sudden end.

"Are you gonna get that, Lizzy?" asked Ryan, trying to capitalize on the distraction.

Lizzy's eyes alternated between Ryan and the phone. "Sure thing, boss. Don't forget choir practice this evening. For everyone, and that includes the both of you." Accepting defeat, she retreated to her nearby desk, sat down, and picked up the receiver. "NYPD, twentieth precinct. Yes, sir. Okay, please give me the details. Yes. Okay. Just one second."

The receptionist turned to Ryan, covering the mouthpiece of the phone with her hand. Her expression turned serious. The atmosphere changed immediately as the real world intervened. "Body over at the harbor. Jogger found it this morning. The harbor boys need some assistance." She returned to the caller, jotting down the details on her notepad.

The detective looked at her inquiringly. "This is my breakfast break. I've got a bagel here somewhere that's waiting for me."

"Ryan, go give the harbor boys a hand!" A booming, gravelly voice sounded from one of the few adjacent offices.

Ryan sighed loudly for effect. "Why, are they a little . . . out of their depth?" He couldn't resist the play on words.

It took Tony a moment to recognize the pun. He broke into a fit of muffled laughter. "Hey, that's pretty funny, boss!"

The chief appeared in the hall, looking thoroughly unimpressed. His massively overweight frame filled the doorway. Sweat glistened on his balding forehead. "Don't get smart. Remember, it's that time of the year. You know, reviews, promotions, and all. I am reading the list, checking it twice. Who's been naughty, who's been nice?"

Ryan knew better than to resist. The chief's word was law, and he ran the department with an iron fist. He was fair, but Ryan knew better than to second guess his orders. He was already putting on his long gray trench coat. "Aw, chief. It's probably just another jumper. There's always a few this time of year. That damn bridge is like a magnet for people."

The chief frowned. "Yeah, well. Bring your sidekick with you. Maybe he can learn something."

Ryan sighed loudly, glancing at Tony with a slight smile playing about his lips. "Tony? Nah, don't think so, chief. We're still stuck on sit and roll over."

CHAPTER 2

Dark Waters

A biting wind greeted the detective and cadet at the harbor quay, throwing snow and sleet in their faces. Ryan pulled the collar of his long coat up around his neck, ducking his head against the cold. The gentle clinking melody of the masts of ships mingled with the cries of seagulls, clustered together for warmth along the harborside railing. From somewhere out in the misty harbor came the distant mournful sound of a foghorn, like some great whale hidden in the depths.

They made their way along the wooden dock to a solitary low building, its white paint weathered and peeling. A faded sign reading "Harbormaster" was just barely legible over a squat door.

Ryan raised his fist to knock and then paused, glancing at Tony. "Okay, Tony. Take notes. Observe. And rule 101 of New York's finest, look as though you know what you're doing."

Tony nodded in response, his teeth chattering. "Got it."

Ryan knocked heavily on the door. There was no

response. He cleared his throat. "NYPD."

He pushed the door slowly as it creaked open in protest.

An elderly man with disheveled white hair and a matching beard sat at a desk in an otherwise spartan room. An electric heater was working hard to keep the chill out of the air. A single window in the wall offered an unobstructed, muted view over the mist-shrouded harbor. The man lowered his spectacles at their approach. "Good day to yar. Glad you came over."

Ryan flashed his police badge. "Morning. Detective Ryan. This is Cadet Vincenti. NYPD. Are you the harbormaster here, sir?"

The man smiled benignly. "Last time I checked. Sorry, yes. That'd be me. Been harbormaster here these last thirty-five years. Yar. These here are my waters. No offense meant."

Ryan edged closer to the electric heater and rubbed his hands. "None taken. Now. We received a call about a body washed up here."

The harbormaster's smile faded, and the color seemed to drain from his face. "Yar. Early this morning. We get a few during the year, you know. Some folk had enough. This time of year can be tough for people. To be alone, I mean."

Ryan considered the man's words for a moment. That was his first guess. Likely some poor city worker who had been dumped unceremoniously by his girlfriend before Christmas. There was always at least one each year. "Yes. And about what time did you discover the body, sir?"

The harbormaster scratched his bearded chin in thought. "Hmm. Just after seven. It was still dark. Just startin' to get bright. My favorite time of day."

"How's that then?" asked Ryan, looking out of the window at the dull bank of fog rolling over the harborside.

The old man shook his head. "Sorry. Little hard of hearing these days. I blame it on one too many damn foghorns."

The detective repeated himself in a louder voice. "Why is that your favorite time of day?"

The harbormaster looked at him in confusion. "What do you mean?"

Ryan sighed. He had a feeling it was going to be one of those days when everything dragged and a simple task would prove to be a knot of stubborn complications. "Never mind. Did you find it?"

"Yar, it's been pretty cold these past few days," said the harbormaster.

Ryan made momentary eye contact with Tony, sharing a "this is going to be a long day" kind of look. The cadet wore a bemused smirk on his face. "O-kay. Did you discover it yourself?"

The old man raised his head to one side questioningly. "What's that then?"

The detective gave up any pretense of trying to avoid hurting the man's feeling and raised the volume of his voice considerably. They weren't getting anywhere. "The body!"

"No need to shout. I'm not deaf yet," answered the

harbormaster. "No. Not me. A jogger found it. Gave him quite a shock, too. He came by with the harbor police. Don't think he'll be running again anytime soon." He gestured out the window towards the edge of the harbor. "Just down there, at the end of the pier."

Ryan was getting somewhere now. "Do you have any tide and current charts of the area, sir?"

"Yar. I surely do. Just a moment." The harbormaster rifled through a drawer in his desk, cursing to himself before he had a eureka moment and triumphantly presented the detective with a large roll of paper.

"Any guess where the body came from?" Ryan continued trying to extract some further information.

The harbormaster mulled over the question. "He seemed like a local man, he probably —"

"No," Ryan interjected. "I meant, was the body washed down from upriver, do you think?"

The old man's forehead wrinkled in thought. "Ah, yar. Hard to say. Depends on how long the body was in the water. Been lots of storms this winter along the Hudson. They upset the tides. You best ask the coroner."

Ryan gathered up the tide charts from the desk. "Can I take these charts with me?"

"Yes," the man answered, returning to his paperwork. "It's in the back. Wipe the seat when you're done, won't ya?"

Ryan sighed and decided to give up while he was

ahead. "I'll be taking these tide charts with me then, sir," he said loudly. "Thank you for your time."

The harbormaster gave Ryan a critical look. "Yar. No need to holler. I can hear ya just fine."

Ryan gave a final courteous nod to the harbormaster and ushered Tony out of the office in front of him. They were met again by the penetrating cold wind. Ryan dumped the tide charts into Tony's arms. "Well, he was helpful," he declared sarcastically. "Here you go, Tony. Let's check out the crime scene for ourselves."

They followed the wooden quay, slick with rain and snow, down to the water's edge. The far bank was half obscured by a veil of fog. The wind was fierce, whipping the detective's hair into his eyes. One side of the railing was cordoned off with yellow police tape, bearing the words: Police. Crime scene. Do not enter." Ryan ducked under the tape and Tony followed close behind him. "Careful now. Don't disturb nothing here."

Ryan surveyed the murky churning waters below, assessing the area. "Not much to see here," he muttered half to himself. "Water here is pretty deep. Well over a hundred feet. Body probably got entangled around the pier supports. Could have been here for days."

He took a tentative step back from the edge of the quay. Being around deep water made him nervous. He was embarrassed to admit that, even to himself. His father had spent most of his life working on or around boats. During Ryan's childhood summers spent on the beaches, his father used to regularly make fun of him, teasing him and threatening to throw him in the water.

Tony elbowed him gently. "What are you thinking, boss?"

Ryan pushed away the slight feeling of illogical panic welling within him and turned his eyes away from the dark water. "I'm thinking if we are lucky, this is out of our jurisdiction."

"How do you mean, boss?" Tony asked.

Ryan continued. "Well. Crime happened upstate, not here in the city. Body floated down here with the winter storms. Maybe a homicide. Hard to say. But it might be someone else's problem."

Tony acknowledged the detective's words. "Any other pearls of wisdom, boss?"

Ryan shivered and turned his back to the harbor and the relentless wind. He rubbed his hands together as he blew into them, trying to restore circulation to his fingers. "Yeah. Don't forget your damn hat in the city in winter! Let's get the hell out of here! I need a coffee."

CHAPTER 3
Sanctuary from the Storm

St. Patrick's Cathedral was sandwiched between two modern tall buildings of glass and concrete in downtown Manhattan. Its ornate neo-Gothic architecture gave the impression of a finely decorated wedding cake, strangely out of place in the jungle of towering skyscrapers that surrounded it. The cathedral always reminded Ryan of a spaceship from another galaxy that had crash landed in the middle of the city.

Ryan's parents were Irish and as a result, he had inherited an unfailing discipline of attending mass early every Sunday morning. It had become part of his habits. He had always been drawn to churches, not because he was overly religious, but because inside the church he could think. His thoughts had enough space to stretch amid the lofty heights of the ceiling.

He believed in a God, sure. It was hard not to when he saw so much horror in his daily work. He needed to have an anchor that reminded him that there was no shadow without light, and each depended on the other for its existence. He usually mentally switched off in mass when the priest began a rambling reading or gospel. He had distilled his beliefs into one simple cardinal rule; he tried to be a genuinely good individual, the kind of person he would enjoy having a coffee with. He figured that the world needed as many good people as it could get its hands on, in order to balance out the depravity that he encountered in his job.

In the oasis within the city, he could let his mind wander and find answers to issues that plagued him. Being a detective meant that he was never really off duty. Often, sitting in the peace of the wooden pews, enlightenment would hit him like an unscheduled freight train rushing out of the darkness. A seemingly unimportant piece of evidence would appear suddenly in his mind and a series of previously unconnected events would make immediate and absolute sense.

There was a peculiar truth to the premise that the harder you tried to make sense of something, the more it eluded you. The same was true of detective work. He would often spend entire mornings and nights poring over case files, only to take a quiet stroll in the park or a visit to the cathedral, and experience abrupt clarity on the motivations behind the crime. Over the last twenty years in his job, he had learned that detective work was not an exact science. It was more like an artist's painting. At first, you had to sketch in the outlines of the entire scene and then, bit by bit, paint in the key objects that told the story: the murder weapon; the motive; the perpetrator; and the fragile threads of evidence that held it all together.

The detective let his thoughts roam, fingering a set of old, worn rosary beads in his pocket. A gift from his departed father. Unseen in a high gallery above, a choir practiced Christmas carols to the tune of an enthusiastic, but slightly off-key, organ. There was another reason he had come to the church; it would be almost three years since his brother died. No, not died, killed in the course of his duty. He turned to the sound of nearby footsteps on the stone floor and the creak of the wooden seat as someone sat down next to him.

"Ryan, what are you doing here?" asked a voice in a thick brogue.

The detective turned to see the middle-aged priest sitting beside him. "Father. What, do I need an invitation now?" he responded with a broad grin on his face. He was always happy to see Father Murphy, a Kerry man through and through, who was as committed to his parishioners as he was to following God's teachings.

The priest returned the smile and clasped his hands together in his lap, as he sat back on the pew. "No, you're always welcome in God's house. I meant I thought you'd be out getting that lovely wife and daughter of yours something nice for Christmas."

Ryan laughed softly. "Yeah. You're right, Father. I just needed to clear my head."

The clergyman sighed and nodded. "You know

that I could tell you it gets easier. That the pain goes away. But I'd be lying. It doesn't, you know. You'll always feel that hole inside you. It makes us human. Means you're still a good man. That you care."

Ryan could feel his eyes sting with tears. He wiped them with the cuff of his jacket. "Ah, Jesus."

The priest gave him a soft playful slap on the back of the head, his face contorted in mock outrage.

Ryan rubbed his head, playing along. "Ow! What did you do that for?!"

Father Murphy leaned closer, a serious expression etched on his face. "What have I told you about taking the Lord's name in vain?"

Ryan swallowed hard. He couldn't ignore the pain welling up inside him. He never spoke to a soul about his brother, not even to his wife. It was too difficult a topic, which words alone just could not do justice. He continued in a soft voice, half broken with emotion. "Sorry, Father. I miss him. I miss him so much. I was the one who encouraged him to join the force. To be one of New York's finest. That's all on me."

The Kerry man digested Ryan's words for a moment. "I know. He was your brother. You were lookin' out for him. He wanted to be just like you. Sure, do ya think he would have even listened to ya if you told him being on the force wasn't right for him?"

The detective let out a long sigh, controlling his breathing again and allowing the emotions to slip away. "Oh, before I forget," he said, reaching for a festively decorated gift bag on the floor next to him. He handed it to the priest. "Here you go. Jameson. Bottle of the good stuff for you. For your nerves and all. Happy Christmas, Father."

The clergyman accepted the gift reluctantly, peering into the bag at the bottle of whiskey. "Ah Jaysus!" he exclaimed softly.

Ryan laughed. "Hey, now you're doing it, too."

The priest laughed out loud. "It's your bad influence, Ryan."

Ryan raised his hands in pretense defeat. "What? Do you want me to take it back to the shop?"

Father Murphy cradled the bag protectively to his chest. "No, no. Wouldn't want to be rude now, would I? I'll find a good home for it. Don't you worry. How are things at the precinct, anyway?"

That was a hard question to answer right now. Christmas was almost here, and a murder had landed on Ryan's desk. "Another poor bastard washed up near pier ninety-nine."

Father Murphy nodded his head in silent agreement. As a priest, he was only too familiar with the depths of despair and loneliness that some people faced at Christmas time. "I'm sorry to hear that. Any ideas?"

Ryan had a few thoughts that were circling in his mind, but nothing concrete yet. "Well, I'm just hoping that it's not one of those Christmas Eve murders. This would be number seven. I need to head over to the coroner's office now."

He stood up in the pew and stretched his

shoulders. Stress seemed to have a nasty habit of gathering in his lower neck.

"How's that new recruit of yours coming along?" the priest asked.

Ryan paused. "Tony. Yeah, bit of a pain in the ass sometimes, but a good kid."

The clergyman winked at him knowingly. "Sounds just like someone I used to know."

Ryan smiled. "Yeah. Well, I better get going. Father."

Father Murphy stood up and took a firm grip of his arm. The detective had the distinct feeling that the priest was trying to channel strength into him for the dark road ahead. "Take care of yourself, Ryan."

Ryan turned to leave. He stopped in mid stride, suddenly remembering the NYPD's annual Christmas Eve carols. "Oh. Don't forget. The precinct's doing carols later this evening."

The priest shook his head. "Since when did you all know how to sing, anyway?"

Ryan gave him a cynical look. "Oh, around about the time the chief figured he'd invite the mayor over. Now it's part of our 'civic cooperation program,' or some other crap." The detective checked his watch. "Oh, gotta run, Father."

Father Murphy watched him hurry down the church aisle, disappearing through the heavy doors in a flurry of snow driven in by a sudden draught of air.

CHAPTER 4

The Body

Ryan hurried along the crowded sidewalks of Manhattan, dodging people as best he could. The heavy snowfall had not deterred the last-minute Christmas shoppers. Festive lights in the shop windows glowed brightly through the flurries of snow, attracting throngs of people like moths to a flame. They spilled in and out of the shops, scurrying in all directions.

The snow fell incessantly on the city. Ryan cursed softly as his black office loafers disappeared into a deep snowdrift, the snow and ice coming in over the side of his shoes and giving his socks a thorough soaking. The pedestrian light turned to red.

He paused at the crosswalk, waiting for the heavy traffic to ease. Lines of yellow cabs floated past, their tires grinding on the compacted ice. The snow gave the city a muted feeling, as though someone had turned its volume down to a more bearable level. It was strange. In all the years he had worked in New York, he had never once had a free Christmas Eve. The magic of the season was all around him and here he was, somehow cocooned inside a bubble of his own making. The metal police badge that pushed against his chest felt unusually heavy under his jacket. He saw someone dressed as Santa Claus ringing a brass bell at the street corner, collecting money for some charity or another. He reached into his pocket and emptied a handful of change into the man's collection box. "Thank you, sir. You have yourself a great Christmas!"

The words echoed in his mind. *A great Christmas.* He'd settle for just making it to Christmas and hanging his jacket up in the hallway. A shiver tingled down his spine. He dismissed it as being due to the bitingly cold temperatures, but he knew what it was. It was what detectives referred to as the "hunch." That mythical beast that often alighted on an experienced detective's shoulder and pointed the way ahead, like a guardian angel who had had a career change. It offered up nothing definite, only a whisper of truth. And like all hunches, it was only possible to truly recognize a hunch when the case was all wrapped up, sealed neatly, and sent to archives to end its days in a dusty cellar under the city streets. He felt as though he was now on the trail of the case, working the leads. It was beginning.

Spotting a break in the traffic, he jogged across the busy street. He looked around him, searching for Tony. He had agreed to meet the cadet somewhere outside the coroner's office. He could feel his energy levels dropping. The freezing weather was fatiguing him. Damn, he could murder a coffee.

"Boss, hey!"

He squinted through the snow, looking down the street to see the cadet waiting for him in the shadow of a building.

Tony offered him a cup of coffee. "Here's your coffee, boss."

"Attaboy, Tony!" he said, wasting no time in taking a long slug from the paper cup. He grimaced as he swallowed. "It's ice cold!"

Tony shrugged apologetically. "Erm. Well, you asked me to be here at ten."

Ryan acknowledged his tardiness. Cold caffeine was better than no caffeine at all. "Sorry. I had some important stuff I had to deal with. Now. You ready to do this?"

Tony nodded and stamped his feet to restore feeling to his toes.

The detective was aware that Tony probably had not had the pleasure of examining many dead bodies up close so far. The cadet was still fresh out of the academy. It was a tough transition, accepting that a body was just a shell and no longer truly a person. It was a trait that separated an experienced police officer from a cadet. Ryan remembered the first victim he had seen. It had involved a particularly gruesome murder in a scrap yard downtown. He was haunted by nightmares about it for weeks afterwards. He had made a mental note to give Tony some moral support and guidance to help him get through the examination.

"'The Star-Spangled Banner,'" Ryan said in a

matter-of-fact tone of voice.

Tony gave him a blank stare.

"Bodies don't look their best when they've been in the water for a few days," the detective offered in explanation. "If you feel funny, try to singing the lines of 'The Star-Spangled Banner.' You'll be fine."

Tony took a moment to process this. "Oh. Yeah. But, boss. I don't think I know that song. I don't even know what that means."

Ryan cupped his hands to his mouth, his breath thawing his fingers. "That's okay. No one does. But if you need to get your mind off the . . . smell and the body, you sing those lines."

Tony seemed to be still digesting this morsel of advice. "Okay, boss."

Ryan put one hand on his shoulder and steered him into the nearby doorway. Security buzzed them through, and the door clanged shut heavily behind them, closing out the hum of the city.

They followed a long corridor, their footsteps echoing in the quiet. The place smelled of antiseptic and a sweet cleaning agent. It always brought to Ryan's mind a hospital ward. A uniformed security guard at a desk looked up from the paper he was reading to give them a cursory nod as they strolled past. The detective paused at a metallic door and rapped softly with his fist before opening it.

The smell of medicinal alcohol was stronger here, almost burning in the nostrils. One side of the room was occupied by a long desk, littered with metallic examination tools. Ryan noticed that a dark suit and tie had been tidily folded and placed in a large see-through evidence bag. Presumably the former trappings from the victim's existence. A man in a long white lab coat and glasses sat next to a naked male body laid out on a table of polished chrome. The man looked up from his work. He had the demeanor of a college professor. "Ah, Detective Ryan. Please excuse me. I'm just finishing up."

The coroner had taken a new tool from his nearby stand and was busily cutting his way through a section of the corpse's abdomen. Never taking his eyes away from his work, he began to talk. "Isn't it fascinating? When the body clock stops ticking, the tissues degrade at a cellular level. Like a fallen apple rotting in the sun." He grunted as he struggled with the tool. There was a wet squelching sound, and the coroner grunted in satisfaction. "It's just a matter of time before nature reclaims what was rightfully hers. Oh, just a moment."

The man dropped the surgical instruments on a neighboring table with a clatter of metal, splattering it with dark blood. He turned to face the detectives, taking off his glasses to give them his full attention. "Are you okay, Detective Ryan? You don't look so . . ."

Ryan could feel his stomach churning, like he was on a roller coaster. The smell of the body this close was a powerful mix of alcohol and undefinable organic odors. The coroner wiped his hands on his chest, smearing a trail of blood and slime across his long white lab coat.

"Hmm. Yes, I'm okay. Thanks." The detective

managed in a weak voice.

Tony appeared close to him. "Boss, you wanna go outside and get some air?"

Ryan tried to shrug off the overwhelming sense of nausea. He cleared his throat. "No. I'm perfectly okay."

Tony turned to view the examination table, edging closer to the corpse. "What's that, sir?" he asked, pointing to a large red organ, which sat next to the body.

The corner swiveled his stool to face the cadet, eager to share his findings. "Ah, yes. They're the lungs. I examined those earlier this morning. Fascinating organ. The lungs were not flooded with water, which is typically the case with a drowning."

Tony chewed his lip. "So the victim was dead before he was thrown in the water?"

The coroner looked impressed with the cadet's deduction. "Oh, yes. Absolutely."

The coroner beckoned for them both to come closer. He pointed a gloved finger to the dead man's head. "Strange bruising here on the forehead. Look, here. A small arrow shape, driven with considerable force, fracturing the cranium. Death would have followed moments thereafter."

Tony stared at the body, lost in thought.

The coroner carefully removed his surgical gloves and picked up a clipboard, which was scrawled with handwritten notes. "Verdict is death by unlawful means. And some unusual punctures across most of the body. I can't quite place the source, but I'll have more for you once I complete my examination. And nylon netting around parts of the victim, like he was caught in a fishing net. Interesting. Environmental contamination, maybe from the Hudson? Male. Mid-thirties. My guess is he'd been in the water for perhaps a week."

Ryan was desperate. "Oh, say can you see," he sang softly to himself, "by the dawn's early light, what so proudly we . . . Ah, damn. I can't remember the rest." Bile welled in his throat. He turned and raced for the door to save himself the humiliation of vomiting all over the coroner's nice clean floor.

The coroner looked up from the body to watch the detective's hurried exit. "Very patriotic chap, that Detective Ryan."

"Yeah. He's a real American," Tony said absent-mindedly, his mind trying to assimilate the implications of the coroner's finding. And then the realization hit him. "Oh, God. Another Christmas Eve murder."

Ryan gulped in fresh air as he held a steadying hand on the outside wall of the building. Tony emerged from the coroner's office wearing a serious expression. "We've got another Christmas Eve murder, boss," he said in an almost apologetic tone.

The detective straightened up and took a long steadying breath. "Damn. Hope you didn't have any plans for this evening then. Let's get back to the station."

Tony hesitated for a moment, as though struggling with himself whether to say something.

"What so proudly we hailed at the twilight's last gleaming."

Ryan wiped his mouth with the cuff of his jacket. "What?"

Tony shrugged. "That's the next line of the song."

The detective gave him a withering look. "Thank you, Cadet Vincenti. I'll be sure to remember that for next time."

"Sure, boss. No problem," said Tony in response.

Ryan shook his head. Sarcasm was totally lost on the kid.

CHAPTER 5
A Breadcrumb

Ryan nursed a cup of steaming coffee in his hands by his desk. The day had done a complete nosedive with the realization that this was yet another murder that fitted neatly into his Christmas Eve Murders case file. He had been holding out a glimmer of hope that it was just another lovestruck jumper that he could wrap up with a report and go home.

All of the bodies had been washed up within the same few square miles of the harbor, on or around Christmas Eve. Sometimes there was one, sometimes there were two. As far as Ryan could tell, there was no logic to the victim count in any given year. But what if they had just found the first body and another one was floating somewhere in the icy waters, hidden from passersby? That was often the pattern with serial murderers. At one point, they lost all sense of inhibition.

"Boss, you got a sec?" Tony appeared next to him with a strained expression on his face. Ryan had seen this look before on the cadet when he was unsure of something and didn't know whether to bring it to the detective's attention, for fear of revealing himself as being clueless or incompetent.

The detective took another tentative sip of the hot coffee. "Sure. You got something for me?"

The cadet shifted on his feet nervously. "Well. Maybe. It might be nothing, but I've been looking over the local tide and current charts for the Hudson. You know, the ones we got from the harbormaster?"

Ryan nodded. "Yeah. Sure," he said encouragingly.

"Well," Tony continued. "I checked all the previous crime scenes over the last few years and well, there seems to be a pattern to where all these bodies come from."

Ryan gently put down the coffee cup on his desk. The cadet had his full attention now.

Tony pointed to a map in his hand, covered with circles scrawled in red pen. "I drew all the results on this map and checked with the historical and tidal data and . . . the source of all this seems to be a ten-mile radius of a location upstate in the Catskills."

Tony waved a see-through evidence bag in the air, which held a small piece of torn cardboard. "And then I checked this piece of paper that was found on the last victim's body. Looks like it came from a box of matches. Most of the ink's been pretty well washed out, but you can still just about make out the words on the back: Stone Ridge. A small village in the Catskills, boss. Almost a hundred miles north of the city."

Ryan's brain was computing this bomb of

information that Tony had just dropped on him. His mind was racing, making connections. This represented a real lead. This was the spark the investigation needed to light the fires of police work. Ryan's earlier hunch was proving right. They were now firmly on the trail. They had found their first breadcrumb.

The detective took the evidence bag carefully, like he was handling a live grenade. This tiny and seemingly insignificant piece of cardboard could hold answers. "Let me have a look at that. You've been busy. Good work, Tony. Really good, work."

Tony blushed from ear to ear. His frame seemed to sag in relief that he had finally done something useful. "Thanks, boss."

Ryan stepped up from his desk. "Let me talk to the chief about this. No. Come with me. This was your hard work."

Ryan led the cadet to the chief's office and knocked respectfully. He opened the door cautiously. The chief was on the phone, but he flagged them to come in anyway as he wrapped up his conversation. "Just give me one minute, fellas."

A moment later, the chief put the phone down slowly. "That was the mayor. The *Times* has already picked up your story on the body in the harbor. They're going to go to town on this. They're calling it a serial killing. God, I hope you've got some good news for me."

Ryan's eyes glinted. They had stumbled on a lead just in time. He cleared his throat. "So, the latest victim's body definitely fits the other Christmas Eve murders. No question. Tony here did some homework, and we have a lead to a little village upstate. What did you say it was called, Tony?"

Tony peered at the evidence bag. "Stone Ridge, boss."

The chief mulled over the name. "Where the hell is that, anyway?"

"Small village in the Catskills. One horse town type of place," Ryan answered.

The chief immediately began dialing the phone. "You boys are taking a trip upstate. I'll call our friends in Ulster County and get a liaison officer to meet you up there. Get something on this. Anything. I don't care. Something I can sell to the mayor, okay?"

Ryan and Tony nodded their understanding in unison and left the chief's office as he made his call to the Ulster County Sheriff's office.

"Get your stuff together, Tony. We're out of here." Ryan put a hand on the cadet's shoulder as he turned to go. "Don't forget your firearm," he said almost in a whisper.

Tony looked shocked. "You serious? What? Up there? What am I gonna need it for? Some mad cow?"

Ryan gave him a stern look to show that this was not a topic for debate, hurriedly grabbed his leather briefcase, and packed away the case file, together with some personal belongings from his desk.

The chief appeared in the doorway of his office.

"Lizzy, darling. Can you get me the keys for a car for Ryan here?"

Lizzy snapped to attention. "Sure." She fumbled through a pile of papers on her desk. "Ryan, you'll need to fill in this requisition form," she said waving a document at the detective.

The chief stormed over to her desk and snatched the papers from Lizzy's outstretched hand. "Here. I'll do that." He lowered his voice, "Just get out of here, okay? Get up there and get out before the snowstorm hits."

Ryan caught the keys that Lizzy threw over to him. "We are out of here," he said struggling to put on his coat.

Lizzy presented him with a baguette sandwich, half wrapped in a brown paper bag. She held it like a peace offering. Ryan guessed that she probably felt guilty about embarrassing him earlier. "Here boys, take my sandwich. It's a long drive up there."

Ryan gladly accepted the food. Lizzy had saved them the inconvenience of having to stop somewhere to get food in the city. He could feel his stomach rumbling already. "You are an angel, Lizzy."

The receptionist gave him her winning smile and winked conspiratorially. "I've been trying to tell you that for years. Take care of yourselves, and Ryan, you keep an eye on Tony for me, will you?"

The remark appeared to sting the cadet. "What are you, my mother?" retorted Tony.

"You see. Like I said, Tony. Lizzy could be your mom." Ryan whispered to him teasingly as they left the busy office.

It was time to follow the breadcrumbs . . .

CHAPTER 6
Road Trip

Ryan stared out of the car's passenger window. The windshield wipers were working overtime, beating a steady rhythm against the glass, pushing away the seemingly endless snowflakes. They were crawling in traffic through icy slush over George Washington Bridge, leading them out of the city. Horns blared up ahead as people lost their patience with the gridlock. On a clear day, they would have been greeted by unparalleled views of the Manhattan skyline, but today the bridge was shrouded in low clouds. It seemed somehow fitting, as though the city itself was shamefully trying to hide the dark deeds of the crime that had been committed.

Ryan turned the dial on the radio, searching for a weather or traffic update. The upbeat voice of a DJ emerged from the hiss and snippets of garbled music. "A severe weather warning has been issued for New York State. The good news is that it's guaranteed to be a white Christmas! Heavy snowfalls of up to eight inches are expected in the city with over a foot in the Catskills. Stay tuned to Westchester radio, folks. We've got some classic songs coming your way over—"

He killed the radio. He'd heard enough. They were literally driving into the eye of the snowstorm. He let out a long sigh. "Damn. I can't believe it's taking this long to get out of the city."

Tony nodded, peering through the windshield, his hands clutching the steering wheel. "Yeah, well. Roads are icy as hell." He started whistling a tune and then stopped abruptly. "Hey, how about a game, boss?"

Ryan gave him a questioning look. "A game?" he asked.

Tony smiled. "Yeah. You know. To help pass the time."

The detective thought for a moment. "A game. Okay. How about 'what the hell is going on here?'"

Tony yawned widely. "It's just Christmas, you know. Holiday traffic and all."

The detective shook his head. "No, I don't mean with the traffic, Einstein. I mean with these murders."

The traffic started to speed up and Tony exhaled sharply with relief. "Hey, maybe this is the big break you've been talking about. You get your promotion and I get my nice shiny silver badge."

Ryan gave a short incredulous laugh. "Yeah, it could be. It could also be the year the chief transfers us both to traffic duty."

Tony seemed genuinely concerned about such an eventuality. "Oh, no. Not that. Anything but that, boss. I hate sitting around in the car. My Uncle Hughie put on ten pounds after his first two months in traffic. He blamed it on the donuts, you know, the ones with the little sprinkles."

Ryan pictured them both sitting on the side of the highway eating donuts with sprinkles and chuckled to himself. "Well, then. Let's make sure that doesn't happen."

"Agreed, boss," said the cadet.

Ryan also disliked being couped up in a car. Being stuck in traffic and inhaling exhaust fumes didn't lend itself well to creative thinking. It suddenly occurred to him that there was actually one useful thing they could do.

"Listen, Tony," he said. "Now is as good a time as any. We need to finish off your review for the year."

Tony shifted uncomfortably in the driver's seat. "Okay. Why not."

Ryan prepared himself. Mentally rolling up sleeves to get some proper answers out of the cadet, so he could file the report and get the appraisal form off his desk. He wasn't altogether sure about how to approach the subject. "You know, we have to talk about your last firearms test."

"Um, hmm," Tony managed in response.

"So," Ryan continued. "Explain to me why you got full marks for all your previous firearms training exercises and then suddenly you get a big fat zero."

Tony remained resolutely silent.

The detective looked out of the window and folded his arms. "I'm listening. And we have until we get to Stone Ridge to get this all sorted."

An awkward silence followed as Tony struggled to find the rights words. "I don't like guns, boss," he managed in a whisper.

The detective blinked in confusion. He thought he might have misheard Tony. His mind struggled for a moment to formulate the right response. "You don't . . ." He stifled a laugh and cleared his throat instead. He had received professional management training on this topic. Apparently, it happened with reasonable regularity on the police force. He pulled himself together. "Sorry, it's just . . . well, police and guns go together like. . ." He sought to find the right analogy, staring at the snowy roadway ahead of them. "Like Christmas and snow."

Tony was getting upset. He was chewing his lip nervously, which Ryan knew was like an early warning sign with the cadet. "I know," he said apologetically. "I can hit the mark every time, but I hate guns. They freak me out, like every time."

Ryan whistled softly through his teeth. He knew he had to tread carefully here. "I had no idea. I thought you were just hung over or something. Listen. Ready for some big news?"

Tony gave the detective a sideways glance.

Ryan knew he had to diffuse this issue without blowing it out of proportion, but at the same time he figured it was up to him as the experienced detective to help Tony get over this reticence in handling firearms. "I don't like guns either. But, and it's a big but. There comes a time in every officer's career when he has to decide what's more important. Saving himself or someone else versus some fear about whether he's doing the right thing by pulling the trigger."

Tony was struggling with the detective's words. "Yeah, I guess so," he said feebly.

Ryan gave the cadet a few moments to let the weight of his words sink in. The traffic had loosened up, and they were gradually leaving the noise of the city behind them. The wide expanse of the I-87 highway opened up ahead of them, framed by trees along the snowy verges.

"I'm gonna ignore your last firearms test report," Ryan declared. "I'm gonna say you had the flu. So, my advice to you is this; don't let this get in your way of making a name for yourself on the force. Get your head ready for that moment. Make it up in your head if you have to. Say it over to yourself if it helps. Don't freeze. Don't ever freeze. You know the handbook: evaluate the situation; assess the risk; and if justified, pull the trigger."

Tony was chewing again on his lip. "Thanks, boss."

Ryan squinted through the fogged-up windshield, trying to read the upcoming road sign behind the thickening snowfall. "Don't miss the next exit for Stone Ridge."

PART II – THE CATSKILLS

Actus non facit reum nisi mens sit rea.

"An act does not make a person guilty,
unless their mind is also guilty."

—Edward Coke (1797), English
jurist, Institutes, Part III.

CHAPTER 7
Welcome to Stone Ridge

Turning off the I-87 revealed the true extent of the snowstorm. While the highway had benefitted from salting and gritting, the secondary roads leading to Stone Ridge were almost impassable. The officers' black sedan inched along country roads buried beneath snow. It was becoming increasingly difficult to tell where the roads ended and began. Everything was covered in a thick white blanket, submerging parked cars and hedges alike. Despite Tony's best efforts, the car frequently slid across the road when the wheels found only a layer of ice under the snow for traction.

The windshield wipers seemed to be on their last legs, groaning loudly against the glass in protest as they struggled to keep up with the sheer volume of snowfall. It had been a while since Ryan could remember seeing a winter quite like this. Looking out at the world transformed into a winter wonderland, he shook his head. How on earth were they going to get back home in time for Christmas?

"There it is!" Tony exclaimed, his voice straining

to be heard over the incessant whine of the wipers.

Ryan glanced out of the window. A large road sign was partially submerged by a hungry snowdrift. The lettering was barely visible through the curtain of snow: Welcome to Stone Ridge.

The detective sat up in his seat for a better view of their surroundings. "Yup. We're here," he agreed. Squinting through the glass, he could see the beginnings of a settlement. Rows of picturesque old colonial houses, with generous plots of land and outbuildings, framed the roadway. Looming ominously behind the village was the shadow of the Catskills mountains, barely discernable behind the veil of falling snow.

"It looks pretty with all this snow," Tony said.

Ryan wasn't impressed. He was a city boy through and through. Having grown up in the confines of the city, wide expanses of space made him somewhat nervous. He felt like a bird that had spent its entire life in a cage, even if someone had left the door open, he would have ignored the world outside. The streets and avenues of the five boroughs of the city represented the known universe to the detective.

"I guess so," he agreed reluctantly. "Keep heading down Main Street." Ryan struggled with a map in his lap. "Sheriff's office should be on the next block."

Tony cursed as the car slid and the back wheels spun wildly, sending the vehicle into a fishtail maneuver. The cadet recovered control after a few awkward moments. "Whoa, it's slippery as hell, boss."

Ryan exhaled loudly. "We have truly left civilization behind."

Something huge appeared in front of them through the pelting snow. "What the hell is that!?"

"What, what do you mean?" Tony demanded, a hint of panic in his voice.

The detective strained to see through the windshield. "Just up ahead. There's something on the road. Turn the car!"

Tony reacted instantly, pumping the breaks and turning the steering wheel as far as it would go. The car skidded into a huge snowbank, and they both sat still for a moment as the engine idled. Somewhere hidden from sight, a cow lowed.

Tony rubbed the windshield with his hand, trying to get rid of the fog of condensation. "Jesus. Was that a cow?" he asked, his voice tinged with an odd mixture of shock and amazement.

Ryan clipped him softly on the back of the head, catching him off guard.

"What the hell, boss?" Tony asked, turning to the detective.

Ryan gave him a look which clearly communicated that he had warned him about cursing already. "Don't be taking the Lord's name in vain. But yeah, it was a damn cow, covered in snow."

Tony sighed deeply before reversing out of the snowbank. "Thanks for the heads-up. I didn't see nothing but snow."

The car crawled down the quaint street, passing many tidy whiteboard houses. "Okay," Ryan declared suddenly, consulting his map. "Here we are. Pull over there. Slowly now. That's the Ulster County Sheriff's office."

Tony killed the ignition, and mercifully, the windshield wipers stopped their frantic rhythm across the windshield. They both sat there in silence, savoring the absence of noise. Tony rested his head back against the headrest and closed his eyes for a moment. It had been a long drive from the city.

They hadn't seen a soul so far in the village. Ryan guessed that the villagers knew better than to venture out in this weather. Stone Ridge had an odd, hushed feeling about it, as though it was holding its breath, waiting for events to unfold. Thinking about it gave Ryan a tingle down his spine. Their lead had drawn them up here to a small town in the middle of nowhere. Could a picture-perfect little town like Stone Ridge hold the key to solving a series of grisly murders? Being here now with the case file tucked into his leather satchel made Ryan question whether they had really read the signs properly. Could an unassuming hamlet of houses huddled together to keep warm in the face of a winter storm actually provide the answers they were looking for?

Ryan gathered his thoughts. "Okay, Tony. Now remember this ain't the city. Folks here might be a little . . . different. Be on your best behavior and we can get in and out of here."

Tony emptied the last few crumbs from the brown sandwich bag that Lizzy had given them into his mouth. "What do you mean 'different'?"

"Erm . . ." Ryan struggled to find the words he was looking for. "Maybe a little . . . slower, you know. Things probably move slower here than in the city."

Tony chewed thoughtfully on the last of the sandwich. "Slower. I can do slower, boss."

The detective grabbed his belongings from the back seat. "Let's go."

Ryan paused for a moment as he got out of the car and glanced around him. He was sure that he felt eyes boring into his back. He braced himself against a sudden gust of snow and ice, his eyes scanning the windows of the nearby houses. Perhaps he was mistaken. He dismissed it. It had been a long drive. They could both do with a break and something to eat. And God, let there be some good coffee.

Unknown to the officers, their arrival in the small town was being watched from a second story window in a weathered old colonial building. The hidden figure was sure of who they were. It was a small town. Outsiders from the city. One older, wearing a gray fedora hat and trench coat, the other younger, and his manner deferential to his superior. The movements of their upper bodies were slightly awkward as they got out of the black unmarked car, a tell-tale sign of concealed firearms. So, the NYPD had graced the village of Stone Ridge with their presence. Things were about to get very interesting.

CHAPTER 8
The Sheriff's Office

The officers closed the heavy door of the office behind them and stepped into a narrow hallway. Old habits were hard to break, and Ryan's mind was already scanning the new surroundings. A solitary jacket hung on one of the coat hooks, and a pair of thick snow boots sat underneath in a pool of gathering water, as the snow and ice melted from the soles. There was a detailed map of Stone Ridge on the wall, with the Sheriff's office highlighted in yellow marker. Below a small wooden bench was an assortment of tools, including recently used snow shovels and traffic cones. *So, there was likely only one person in the office right now*, thought Ryan.

They stamped their feet on the frayed welcome mat to remove the excess snow and entered the office area.

"Hello?" Ryan called loudly. "Anyone—" he stopped mid-sentence. Ahead of them, the hallway opened up into a cramped room. A single duty desk was hemmed in by shelves, bursting with an assortment of files. A young lady sat behind the desk in a neat police uniform, crouched behind a typewriter. She glanced up at them through her thick horn-rimmed glasses as the officers approached. "I'm afraid the sheriff is out on a call," she said apologetically. "High priority. One of Old Man Johnson's cows has escaped, again." She looked at the detectives, chewing her gum.

Ryan and Tony exchanged knowing looks, but Ryan thought better of mentioning their run-in with the cow on Main Street. He wasn't sure if they had actually hit the animal or not. Better not start off on the wrong foot.

Ryan introduced them both. "Erm. I'm Detective Ryan, and this is Cadet Vincenti." He paused for a moment, hoping that this would be sufficient to give the police officer a cue as to why they were there. The lady stared at them blankly, continuing to chew her gum.

"We're with the NYPD," Ryan offered. "Our chief called your sheriff earlier today for someone to assist us with our investigation."

She stopped chewing her gum suddenly, an expression of realization spreading across her face. "Sorry, oh. Oh. Yeah! The sheriff told me you'd be coming. Gee, I thought you fellas would be ... bigger. Anyway. Awful really. A body in the harbor. On Christmas Eve, an' all. I'm Cindy. It's nice to meet you fellas. I'll be your liaison officer during your visit."

Ryan nodded. At least they were getting somewhere. Cindy began shuffling through piles of paper on her desk. "Well, let me get you sorted. I'm afraid we don't have much free office space here. Just enough for me and Lucy. And the sheriff's office," she said, pointing to a closed door across the hallway. "So, you'll need to get yourselves set up at the Wynkoop Hotel. It's a nice place. Even George Washington stayed there, I believe. Did you know that?"

"No. I did not, Cindy," answered Ryan, trying to look suitably impressed. He also wanted to give the cadet an example of how to demonstrate patience and restraint while dealing with the villagers.

"It's just a few blocks down the street," said Cindy.

Ryan sighed. He was hoping to have the chance to speak to the sheriff directly, but he would gladly accept the offer of a room in the local hotel. It would be good to have some peace and quiet to formulate their plan of investigation for Stone Ridge. "You mentioned Lucy? Is she your colleague?"

Cindy burst into a fit of childish giggles. It took her a moment to get herself back under control. "Oh, no, no, no! That's our office mascot. Lucy has been with us for some time now. Haven't you Lucy? Lucy!? Now . . . where is she?"

Ryan glanced around the room, expecting to see a dog bowl to provide some clue about the mascot. Cindy continued rifling through her desk. She stopped abruptly with a grin beaming on her face as she held up a plush cow with a small red ribbon around its neck. It looked as though it had seen the worse for wear and one of its button eyes was slightly askew, giving it a somewhat crazed look.

Cindy tilted it from one side to the next and it made a low mechanical mooing sound. She stopped and looked at them for dramatic effect, appearing to be very pleased with herself.

Ryan had to exercise restraint again and not say something smart that might offend the young police officer. He bit his lip to stop himself. "Eh. That's a . . . cow?" Ryan hazarded a guess.

Cindy appeared crestfallen. "Oh, no. Not just any cow. This here is handmade with local materials from Old Man Johnson's farm. Say, if you haven't already got your Christmas presents all sorted out, you might want to visit the farm shop." She gave Ryan a knowing wink. "They sure have some great gifts! Local produce. Support our county, you know."

Ryan nodded, fighting the urge to say something cynical. He could see out of the corner of his eye that Tony was watching him closely. "Hmm-mm. Okay," he managed.

Cindy's hands hovered over the desk, as though she was trying to locate something. "Oh, almost forgot," she declared loudly. "Here it is. Did my homework, you know. List of all the places and people you might want to speak to. Shouldn't take too long. It's a small town." She proffered a handwritten list to Ryan, looking immensely proud of her work.

Ryan took the papers with a smile of gratitude. His eyes ran through the list of names and localities. This was exactly what he needed. Maybe he had misjudged her. She was a little eccentric, but her mind was sharp enough and she appeared to be committed to her job. "Let's see. That's perfect, Cindy. Tony, let's get moving with this." Ryan glanced again at the list. "First stop, the Orchard Diner on Main Street. Thanks, Cindy. You've been a real help."

She laughed nervously, her eyes dropping to the floor in embarrassment. "Why sure. Glad to help you city boys out. Take care now! Weather is pretty bad out there!"

The detectives turned to go. "Pretty bad" was a profound understatement. Looking through the sheriff's office window onto Main Street, it seemed as though the world had disappeared under a sea of brilliant white cotton.

CHAPTER 9

The Orchard Diner

The baguette that Lizzy the precinct office administrator had donated to the detective's cause, had only gone so far. It was just after one o' clock in the afternoon and although the sandwich had kept the hunger pangs at bay, Ryan was now fantasizing about a killer cup of coffee. He hoped that a suitable sugary accompaniment would also provide the boost he needed to get through their investigations in Stone Ridge by the time the day came to a close.

They left the car outside the sheriff's office since the Orchard Diner was just a short walk through the snow. The café occupied a prime position at a corner intersection and was in keeping with the quaint old weatherboard buildings in the village. Ryan pushed the door of the diner open and a little bell behind it rang cheerfully, alerting staff that they had new customers.

Inside was a hive of activity. Most of the tables seemed occupied, and the waitstaff dressed in uniforms reminiscent of American diners in the 1950s hovered dutifully in the aisles. There was a faint smell of coffee lingering in the air, mixed with the scent of meat frying.

Ryan breathed the smell in deeply, his nose and palate evaluating the coffee. "It ain't Valentino's, but let's get ourselves some coffee," he said to Tony as he surveyed the busy establishment.

Tony groaned. "I'm starved."

The cadet was as thin as a rake but had an insatiable appetite. Every time Ryan saw him in the office, he was chewing on one snack or another.

A cheerful waitress appeared from nowhere and gave them a beaming smile. "Hi there, fellas. You need a table?"

Ryan had to muster a measure of self-control to ignore the impulse of responding with some smart-ass retort. He so badly wanted to say that he already had a table at home, thanks, and he had become quite attached to it. Instead, he settled for "Hi. Yeah. That'd be great."

The waitress grabbed a couple of menus. "If you gentlemen would care to follow me, please." She stopped at a table next to the window with a clear view of the wintry street outside. "Now, how about here, with a view of historic Main Street?"

"That's perfect. Very nice," Ryan said charitably.

Tony frowned as he gazed out of the window into the blizzard. "Really, I can't see a thing."

Ryan gave him a nudge with his foot, reminding him of his earlier promise to be mindful of the way people did things here in the village. He tried for an immediate course correct. "But it sure is a very nice town. Lots of . . . snow."

Ryan gave him an unhappy glance, indicating that he expected the cadet to do better than that next time.

The waitress ran a hand through her auburn hair that she wore tied neatly back from her face and took out a small note pad and pen from her apron pocket. "Well, I'm Debbie, by the way, and I'll be taking care of you gentlemen today. Now, what can I get you?" Her speech sounded thoroughly rehearsed. Ryan wondered how many times she had said this so far, just today.

Ryan gave her a smile. She was very polite, and he appreciated politeness. "We'll have two coffees. Both black with sugar. Can you recommend something to eat?"

The waitress considered the question for a moment. "Sure. The pear pie is to die for."

Ryan noticed her choice of words. For a moment, time seemed to pause as his brain worked overtime. They were closing in on their target now. He had to be sure that he registered everything around them. Every little seemingly irrelevant clue could determine whether they found the next lead. The waitress seemed very aware of her surroundings and was good with people. She would be an ideal person to assist them with their investigation.

"The pie is freshly made with pears from Old Man Johnson's farm," Debbie finished.

Ryan pushed his thoughts aside. "Oh, is that so? Okay, then two slices of your finest pear pie."

The waitress appeared to be sizing them up. "Do you want whipped cream with that?" she asked.

As Ryan shook his head in refusal, Tony said, "Yes," enthusiastically.

Ryan laughed. He didn't want to deprive Tony of his daily calorie intake. "Sure, why not. Listen, Debbie. We're with the NYPD. Would you have time for a few questions?"

The waitress scrunched up her face in confusion. "NYPD? Is that like a radio station?"

The detective raised his eyebrows in what he hoped was an expression of the seriousness of the situation. "Eh, no, Debbie. We're with the New York Police Department. We're conducting an official investigation here in Stone Ridge." He paused to let his words sink in. He was only too aware that a lot of people were distrustful of police.

The waitress gasped and gave him a horrified look. "Oh, no. It's about that parking ticket, isn't it? I knew it. I told Sammy we should just pay it and—"

"No. Nothing like that. We just have a few questions. That's all."

She managed a nervous little laugh. Ryan could see that she was unsure of what was expected of her.

Ryan tried to reassure her that it was standard procedure. "If it's okay, maybe you could get us our coffee and pie and we can all sit down here together? Shouldn't take long at all."

She responded hesitantly, as though thinking over the request. "Sure. I guess so. I'll be back in a jiffy."

Ryan watched her go. She glided through the aisles with practiced ease and disappeared from view through a service door designated "Staff Only."

He tapped his fingers on the table. Priority one had been taken care of. Coffee and sustenance were on the way. "Okay, Tony," he kept his voice low, so as not to be overheard. "This is the busiest place in town. People coming through here all the time. And it's the only place to get something to eat for the next ten miles. So, if anyone has seen some people that don't belong here, it'll be Debbie."

Tony glanced around the busy diner. "That makes sense, boss." He looked thoughtful for a moment. "Pear pie? I wonder why not apple pie."

Ryan gave him a serious look. Tony's stomach had now commandeered his brain. The detective had seen it many times before. The kid would be okay once he ate something. "Are you listening to me at all?"

The cadet gave him an apologetic shrug. "Sure, boss. Just hungry is all."

The detective continued. "So, you take the notes. Keep up with me, okay?"

Tony seemed even more distracted. Ryan assumed that some other part of the lunch menu had caught his attention. "Sure. I got this," Tony answered not looking up. "Eh, boss. Look at this!"

Ryan was just about to reprimand him and deliver his usual speech about how it was his time to learn, and if he didn't, he would likely end up archiving paper for the rest of his career. But he was cut short in his tracks as Tony took a small box from the center of the table and gave it a gentle shake. It was a box of matches.

Ryan opened his mouth to say something but was genuinely speechless. The detective took the matchbox carefully from the cadet and turned it over in his hand. One side had a sketch of the colonial building, which the diner occupied, while the reverse had the name of the diner and the address, including at the bottom the words "Stone Ridge." He blinked a few times, making sure that his eyes were not playing tricks and re-examined it. There was no question about it, this was definitely an intact version of the evidence discovered on the last victim. They had only retrieved a fragment of the cardboard from the body in the harbor, but this was the complete, undamaged version of the matchbox.

Ryan whistled through his teeth. "Oh, my God! That's the matchbox that was found on the last victim in the harbor. I know I don't say this often, Tony. But you, you are a genius!"

Their moment of triumph was interrupted as the waitress appeared, weighed down with a heavy tray, carrying their steaming mugs of coffee and two of the biggest slices of pie that Ryan had ever seen. Tony's eyes were immediately drawn to the food. It seemed a fitting reward for Tony's moment of brilliance.

"And here we are," the waitress said, laying down the food and drinks in front of them. "Your coffees, gentlemen, and your pies. With whipped cream."

Ryan gave her a look of thanks and gestured for her to sit down opposite them. She looked uncomfortable as though she was committing an unforgiveable faux pas by sitting in a seat dedicated for paying patrons only.

Ryan took the hot cup of coffee to his lips, inhaling a waft of its nuances. His brain did a quick analysis. Simple but nice. No pretentious illusions. This was a cup of coffee that was made to keep people buzzing along with their day. He took a tentative sip, and his body gave him a euphoric nod of thanks. He could already feel his mind firing up again, shaking off the fog of fatigue. "Okay, Debbie. So how long have you been working here?"

Debbie thought for a moment. "Hmm. Six years, give or take a few months."

Six years, Ryan noted mentally. That would align nicely with the case file he had. The murders had been occurring for the last six years. This was victim number seven. He continued. "And I guess you know everybody in town? I mean by sight at least, right?"

The waitress straightened her apron. "Sure. Of course. This is the best diner in town."

"This is the *only* diner in town," Tony said softly as he scribbled notes down. Ryan gave him an unseen kick under the table.

Ryan cleared his throat to mask Tony's unhelpful statement. "And I suppose if any strangers come in here, they'd stick out. You'd notice them immediately, right?"

"Oh, sure," Debbie said in response. "I mean, most people are locals. Then there's the usual truck drivers. Over there." She indicated discreetly to a table in the corner, where a group of somewhat bedraggled men were tucking into plates heavily laden with fried food. "With their caps and . . . well . . ." She struggled to find the right words. "Usually a bit unshaven, if you know what I mean? But nice folks all the same."

Ryan surveyed the far table to confirm that her description of them had been accurate. "Sure. Goes with the job, I guess. Anyone else that has stood out?"

Debbie placed a hand under her chin in thought. "Hmm. We get a few tourists, with their cameras and all. It's a lovely town, you know. And there's great walking country here in the Catskills. But that's usually in summer. Hmm."

Ryan pushed her gently. "Anything that seemed strange to you? Out of the ordinary, you know?"

The waitress glanced out of the window at the falling snow, lost in contemplation. "Hmm. Well. I don't know if it's anything, but sometime before Christmas each year, we get some very . . . official looking people coming in here. Usually in suits and ties. Real formal, like they're going to a funeral or something. I don't know who they are. They were here just last week. They kept talking about a 'facility.' But I don't know what they meant. Oh, and a local man, Doctor Stewart joined them. He's the veterinarian here in town. He neutered Mister Tom.

My cat."

Another sprinkling of clues to add to their growing list. "That's great, Debbie." Ryan couldn't resist. The coffee had given him a new injection of energy. "Well, maybe not for your cat, though. Er. Facility? Hmm. Okay, Debbie. We will not take up any more of your day."

Ryan pushed the chair aside and stood up. He left a series of dollar bills on the table. "And if I may say so, that pie was the best I've ever tasted. You keep the change."

The waitress smiled warmly in gratitude. "Thanks, gentlemen. You have yourselves a great day in Stone Ridge!" she called after them as they made their way to the exit.

Ryan paused at the door as they took their jackets from the coat stand. "Interesting. Did you get all that?"

Tony struggled with his jacket. "Yeah, but I mean, I've had better pie, even my mama—"

The detective gave him an impatient look. "Not about the pie. I meant, did you get everything she said down on paper? And put that box of matches in an evidence bag."

The cadet tapped his pen on his notepad. "Yes, boss. All here in my little black book."

Ryan put a hand on the door, readying himself before they returned outside to the snowstorm. "Good. Let's make sure Doctor Stewart is on our to-do list." He checked the time on his wristwatch. "Alright, we better hurry if we are gonna make it to the library before they close."

CHAPTER 10
The Public Library

The wind whipped around the officers as they trudged through the heavy snowdrifts, their feet searching for the hidden steps that ran up to the impressive double doors of the public library. The library was an imposing edifice, borrowing from the style of the other colonial buildings in town, except that an aura of faded glory hung about it. The entrance was framed on either side by slim columns, holding up a shingled porch that seemed to sag under the weight of freshly fallen snow.

They closed the doors quietly behind them, glad to be out of the storm. "Pretty grand place for such a small town, don't ya think?" Ryan commented as he removed his hat and brushed it off with his hand.

Tony stamped his feet in the atrium. His footsteps echoed through the high ceilings of the hall. The library seemed deathly quiet, almost like a somber mausoleum. The effect was enhanced by a stained-glass window, allowing a meager level of light into the hallway. *The silence was to be expected*, thought Ryan. It was a library after all, and who goes to the library on Christmas Eve?

From the atrium, the hallway opened into a wide corridor with several doors leading off in different directions. A small brass sign on the wall indicated the available rooms: Main Library; Study Rooms; and Administration. The air was thick with an odor that reminded Ryan of a museum, a heavy scent that had been brewing over decades, probably from the volumes of moldy books. The library held the collective knowledge of decades. The detective was sure that they could learn something useful here.

Ryan paused for a moment and searched his list titled "Persons of Interest" that Cindy from the local sheriff's office had given to him.

Tony joined him, looking bored. "Hey, you wanna hear something funny? The chief was sounding off —"

"Shh." He was interrupted by a stern-faced woman with silvery hair, styled in a bun. She had materialized from nowhere, like an apparition. "Young man, this is a library, not a bar! If you want to yell, please go outside."

Tony nodded and took a tentative step backwards. "Sorry, I didn't mean to . . ."

Ryan guessed that he had found his next person of interest, but from the headmistress-type bearing of the lady, he knew that he would have to be as respectful as possible if he wanted to extract any useful information. "Could you help us, please, ma'am? We are looking for Mrs. Baxter, the head librarian here."

Mrs. Baxter's strict demeanor softened slightly. "Ah, that would be me."

Ryan introduced them both. "We're from the New York Police Department." He flashed his badge and motioned for the cadet to do the same.

The librarian nodded as she examined their police badges. "Ah, yes. Cindy told me you would be paying me a visit. Why don't you come this way into my office?" She gave them a backwards glance as she pushed open a nearby door. "I expected you boys from the city to be . . . well, maybe bigger?"

Ryan sighed and gave Tony a jaded look. "Yeah. We get that sometimes."

Mrs. Baxter led them into her office. It seemed as though they were back in the 1930s. The room had the appearance of an antique shop. A heavy mahogany desk took center stage, in the middle of the room on a frayed woven mat. The floor-to-ceiling shelves in the room were adorned by files and neat boxes lettered from A to Z. The detective assumed this was a card indexing system to catalog all of the library books. This was someone with an orderly mind. *Good*, he thought. *Perhaps there was another piece of the jigsaw puzzle lurking somewhere in this dusty old building.*

The librarian had clearly been expecting them and unrolled a large map on the desk, gesturing for them to take a seat, while she placed a pair of thick reading glasses on the bridge of her nose. "Cindy said that you might be interested in a little local information to give you the lay of the land here," she explained, her eyes scanning the map.

Ryan bent close to the document. "Yes, ma'am. That would be very helpful."

Mrs. Baxter pinned the corners of the map to the table with a collection of paperweights and leaned back in her chair, with a slow creak. "Stone Ridge's humble beginnings can be traced back to the early seventeenth century, with the arrival of the Dutch settlers. George Washington himself once stayed here in our fine town. Did you know?"

Ryan shot Tony a brief look and nodded for the librarian to continue.

The librarian ran her hand lovingly over the map. "Currently, it's home to around eight hundred folks, and really, it's all about either agriculture or tourism these days." She pointed with a crooked finger to a location on the map. "If you look here, you can see Main Street cuts the town neatly in half."

Ryan studied the map. *A small town*, he thought to himself, *with some dark secrets*. "So, farming and tourism keep this place going?"

The librarian agreed sagely. "Yes, sir. Old Man Johnson's farm is one of the main enterprises here. The property covers hundreds of acres. It's mostly dairy farming, but they also have some large tracts of land for growing Douglas fir trees."

"Douglas fir trees," repeated Ryan. "Aren't they Christmas trees?"

"Yes, indeed they are," continued Mrs. Baxter. "It's big business in the city. They grow them up here and then cut them down in December. Transport them downriver to Manhattan in commercial barges. The farm can barely keep up with demand. The Douglas fir tree is the trademark of the farm. It's on all of its locally produced goods."

Ryan's brain absorbed this fact, mulling it over in his mind. There it was: a connection between Stone Ridge and the city.

The detective checked to see that the cadet was keeping up with the conversation and duly taking notes. "Interesting. And is there a real Old Man Johnson still about?"

The librarian chuckled. "There most certainly is. Mr. Johnson is . . ." she glanced around to make sure that they were alone. "Well, he's getting on a bit though now. He's still regarded as somewhat of a local hero. I understand his son-in-law, Doctor Stewart, runs the farm these days."

The name rang a bell. They had heard it earlier today from the waitress in the Orchard Diner. "Doctor Stewart? That's the veterinarian, right?"

"Yes, that's correct," she answered. "Mr. Johnson is a generous patron of this library. He's upstairs in the private members' room, if you'd care to talk to him. Comes here every day to read the local papers."

Ryan's thoughts were racing. That would be perfect. They would get two interviews done at the library alone. He had already planned that he would have to arrange to meet Old Man Johnson separately at the farm.

"Yes, ma'am," Ryan answered. "That would be very helpful."

The librarian removed her reading glasses, which fell on a chain around her neck. "Please follow me." She led them up a wide flight of wooden stairs, their footsteps reverberating loudly through the silent building. The steps were uneven and leaned at odd angles, giving the detective the dizzying sensation that they were on an old ship. She stopped in a hallway adorned with oil portrait paintings. Ryan felt their watchful gaze as they passed by and noted that a few of them had Johnson as their surname. It looked as though Old Man Johnson came from an impressive pedigree. Ryan straightened his tie.

The librarian turned to Ryan with her hand on the door. "Please don't detain him too long, detective," she said in a hushed tone before rapping gently on the door.

They entered into a grand room with several leather armchairs clustered around a large fireplace, in which a log fire crackled cheerily. The impression that they had gone back in time was even stronger here. Several walls were lined with shelves of leather clad volumes, and dark oil paintings of bucolic scenes decorated the room. The air of the room was pervaded by an incessant ticking, emanating from a towering grandfather clock on one side of the room. The detective found it oddly hypnotic, matching his own heartbeat and counting down the seconds of his life. Counting down their time here in Stone Ridge.

The librarian leaned over the only armchair that was occupied. An elderly man appeared to be engrossed in reading a paper and did not acknowledge their presence. "Mister Johnson? There are some gentlemen here to speak to you."

The old man looked up from his paper and gazed at Ryan. His pale gray eyes seemed lost for a moment as though he was emerging from a dream. He grunted and gave a soft laugh. "Huh? NYPD? The boys in blue. New York's Finest, eh? What are doing so far from home?"

Ryan sat down across from him and gestured for the cadet to take the last empty seat. "Sir, we are investigating a series of homicides. We have reason to believe that Stone Ridge may hold some answers for us."

The clock sounded loudly in the silence as the old man considered the question. *Tick-tock. Tick-tock.*

Mr. Johnson smiled. "A little place like this? Are you sure?"

Ryan nodded. "Yes, sir. We believe so. Could I interrupt your day to ask you just a few questions?"

The vacant haunted look appeared in the man's eyes again. "I saw him once, you know," he said slowly in a dreamy voice.

A confused expression spread across the detective's face. "Who would that be then, sir?"

The old man's eyes became fixed at a point somewhere in front of him, as if he was witnessing something unfold before him that only he could see. "One evening as the sun set over the meadows. A figure with a scythe. Walking real slow, across the fields." His gaze seemed to refocus as he returned to the present and glanced up at the detective. "I know I don't have long left for this world. But living is a habit that's so hard to quit." He gave a soft wheezy laugh, which ended in a dry cough.

Ryan hesitated. He had to tread carefully. The elderly man might hold another clue for them. "I see," he said respectfully. "And do you run the farm yourself, sir?"

Mr. Johnson pondered the question for a moment and then in answer, he held up his wrinkled hands, twisted from rheumatism. "Do these hands look as if they could lift the locks on the boundary gates? One of my own bulls trampled me years ago. Biggest damn bull you ever saw. I never recovered fully. To this day, I still don't understand what the hell happened. It's all a blur." He closed his eyes for a moment as he wrestled with the memory. "I gave up doing any real labor seven years ago. My son-in-law takes care of it all now. The farm, the facility, and the business."

There it was. Another echo from earlier. The word "facility" hung in the detective's mind. He looked at Tony, and he could see that the cadet had registered its importance, too.

"You mean the veterinarian? Doctor Stewart?" asked Ryan.

The old farmer nodded and turned his attention to the crackling fire. "That'd be him."

Ryan knew he had to proceed with caution. Mr. Johnson appeared to have one foot firmly in the past and one foot reluctantly in the present. Memories could be a fragile thing. One false move and the whole house of cards could collapse.

"Sir, you mentioned the 'facility.' Could you kindly tell me what you mean?"

"The facility is where we manage the livestock from," Mr. Johnson said in a matter-of-fact tone. "It's an outbuilding up on the pastures. We tend to all the livestock there. Worming. Calving. Tagging. Medical checks."

Ryan needed to push the old man just a bit more. He could sense that they were onto something here. There was a feeling like electricity in the air. "I see. And do you ever get any visitors to the farm? To the facility?"

The elderly man's brow furrowed. The effort of recalling events from the past seemed to be fatiguing him. "Well, now. Let me think," he said as he stared unblinking at the flames licking a blackened log in the fireplace. "About once a year, I think. We get a visit from the state officials checking that everything is hunky-dory, in order, you know. Livestock is healthy, everything is in line with federal and state laws. All that bureaucratic crap." His eyes defocused and remained fixed on the dancing flames. The detective sensed that they were losing him.

"I took on the farm from my Daddy sixty years ago. The world was a different place back then. Things were black and white. We bred cattle, worked the land. Now you need to have a piece of paper for every cow, for every person, for every piece of machinery . . ."

Ryan's mind was turning over the facts. A visit to the facility once per year by people wearing ties. The same people that showed up at the diner in town. Ryan recalled the dark suit and tie the victim had worn, folded neatly in the coroner's examination room.

"I understand," Ryan said. "Sounds just like our precinct office. You've been a real help to us, Mister Johnson. Thank you. I wish you a pleasant day, sir. I hope that we haven't taken up too much of your time."

Ryan got up to leave and Tony followed him.

"I hope you find the answers you're looking for," sounded the old man's tired voice as they left the room.

Answers. Perhaps not answers so much as more breadcrumbs leading the way. The veterinarian Dr. Stewart had now moved right up to the top of their list.

CHAPTER 11
The Veterinarian's Office

The detective and cadet made their way along Main Street, stumbling through deep snow. The town of Stone Ridge was slowly disappearing under heavy white drapes. All color had been leached from the surroundings, and it was difficult to discern where the horizon line ended and the sky began. It reminded Ryan of being woken from a dream, caught halfway between the waking and sleeping world. He almost expected his next footstep to not find solid ground, but instead swallow him into a white void of nothingness. The thought made him feel light-headed.

The deserted streets had an otherworldly atmosphere to them, hiding their secrets behind a blinding radiance. Great mounds of snow piled on submerged cars and hedges loomed out of the thickening flurries of snowflakes. In the trees of the deserted gardens and the gables of the pretty houses, a wind howled mournfully.

It was as though the town had set itself against them, closing its avenues from their prying eyes beneath a white body bag of snow. Ryan cursed as he slipped into a deep drift, soaking his socks through. *That was the second time today*, he thought, and wondered whether he had another pair of socks with him. *What a way to spend Christmas Eve*, he thought glumly. Did he really expect to be able to find any trail in this damn blizzard? This was a wild goose chase, designed for the purpose of appeasing the mayor. He pulled his hat down over his forehead to shield his eyes from the storm as he squinted to survey their surroundings.

The small cottage at number sixteen Main Street appeared like a ghost out of the pale world around them. It stood alone between two larger buildings, in what must have been a well-kept garden. The snow blanketed hedge encircling it looked like the protective arms of a giant. Someone had cleared a path from the garden gate to the doorway. It had been done recently by the look of it. Ryan grabbed Tony by the arm and pointed to the building. The cadet grunted in reply.

Ryan opened the gate, and a small bell rang cheerily, heralding their approach. He walked up the cleared path to the blue painted front door and rubbed off the layer of ice on the metal nameplate on the nearby wall to reveal: Dr. A. Stewart, Veterinarian. By appointment only.

The officers took shelter under the front porch roof. It afforded a welcome respite from the pounding snowflakes and incessant wind.

"Doctor Stewart!" Ryan bellowed over the wind,

as he banged heavily on the cottage door with the wrought iron lion's head knocker. There was an uncomfortable silence, broken only by the sound of the wind in the twisted trees in the garden.

He tried again. "Doctor Stewart! It's the police. We need to talk to you." Ryan and Tony's eyes met. Was it a coincidence that there was nobody here? Or, was someone evading them? The detective could feel a small tingle run down his spine. He had learned to trust his instincts over the years. There was something not quite right here.

The cadet tugged urgently on the sleeve of Ryan's trench coat. "Boss, did you see that?! The curtain just moved. I could swear there was somebody there."

Ryan's mind debated forcing open the door to the cottage, but there was nothing to justify such a measure and it would only get him into trouble with the chief and likely buried in paperwork for the next year. He accepted defeat, for now.

The detective took one last glance at the nameplate near the door and turned to the garden gate. "Okay, we still need to speak to the elusive doctor. Let's get over to the motel that Cindy reserved for us and review what we have."

There it was again. That icy chill down Ryan's back. A sense that their departure from the cottage garden was being watched by someone hidden. He could feel it. Things were in motion now. The wheels were turning, grinding slowly to their inevitable conclusion. Ryan just was not sure where it would lead them.

From the shadows of the hallway in the cottage, a figure watched them disappear into the storm.

CHAPTER 12
The Wynkoop Hotel

The Wynkoop Hotel was a sprawling old colonial building, constructed from gray limestone bricks and occupying a large plot in the center of the historic town. Even through the sheets of incessant snow, the Christmas decorations in the windows shone brightly. Someone had taken the trouble to decorate the gardens with long chains of lights, hung along the trees and front porchway. It looked like a scene out of a fairy tale. Ryan half expected to see a white rabbit rush by with a stopwatch.

Their car was parked in the adjoining street and was almost completely enveloped by the snow. It took Tony a few minutes to dig enough away from the passenger door to allow him to gather all of their belongings and case file documents.

Ryan clapped the cadet on the back as he emerged triumphantly from the car holding the detective's worn leather briefcase. "I knew there was a reason I brought you along," he said grinning.

The pathway of paving stones leading to the main entrance of the hotel was meticulously cleared of snow. A sign in the front garden, which had recently been rescued from a snowdrift read: Vacancies, and underneath that written by hand was the festive message: Come in and try our Christmas eggnog!

As they opened the door, a little bell rang above the doorway. *The locals seemed to have a fascination with bells*, thought the detective as he clumsily patted the snow off his shoulders and entered the warmth of the hotel. There was a lingering smell of cookies and coffee. The detective breathed it in deeply with an expression of approval. "Good day, sir! Wow, I have never seen so much snow!"

An elderly man with a tidy white beard and matching hair sat behind the front reception desk. He gave them his full attention and removed his reading glasses. "Good day? You think? Well, not such a great day out there. Oh, just a moment, fellas. Here's the weather report."

He fumbled with the controls of a radio and the volume blared. "My, oh my, folks. The mother of all snowstorms is here. The I-87 is gridlocked and impassable, both citybound and upstate. Many vehicles have been abandoned on the roadway. We are receiving reports of record snow accumulations in the Catskills. Higher elevations are reporting up to eighteen inches of the white stuff. I think it's safe to say that all minor roads are completely off limits. Visibility is reduced to twenty feet . . ."

The hotel manager clicked off the radio and gave them a sympathetic look. "Well, now. Hope you boys packed a change of clothes. You could be here a while."

Ryan sighed. "We're still planning to get home to the city for Christmas. Miracles do happen sometimes, right?"

The man gave them a skeptical look. "Well, if you say so."

"I'm Detective Ryan, with the NYPD," he said introducing himself. "This is Cadet Vincenti," he added gesturing to his younger colleague.

The man interrupted their polite exchange with a raised hand. "Oh, Detective Ryan. Before I forget. Cindy from the sheriff's department came by earlier with some paperwork for you."

He handed Ryan a tidy pile of documents, tied with a red ribbon and a room key.

"Here you go. I've reserved room 104 on the ground floor over there for you. It's one of the biggest rooms we have. Should give you some privacy. Not that we're busy right now. Oh, and your station chief called, asked whether you could call him back as soon as you arrive."

"Thanks. Is there a phone I can use in the room?" Ryan asked.

"Sure thing," answered the hotel manager. "Now, can I get you boys some tea or coffee."

The detective perked up at the offer of coffee. It had been on his mind the moment he entered the hotel. "Coffee would be great."

"You go get yourself set up then. Anything you need, just holler," said the hotel manager as he busied himself making coffee in the adjoining kitchen.

They made themselves as comfortable as possible in the hotel meeting room. It was far bigger than they needed to serve as a temporary incident room. It had a long dark wooden table and seating for at least a dozen people. The floor-to-ceiling windows afforded a view over the landscaped gardens. The raging storm outside was muted behind the thick glass windows, and the snow fell serenely, gathering on benches arranged near a weathered bird bath.

They had sketched out what little information and leads they had on a large whiteboard. Ryan sat lost in thought, glancing alternatively at the web of hand-written connections on the board, and then back to the garden.

He picked up a doily and put it underneath his coffee cup, muttering to himself. "Not bad. Kind of quaint, I guess."

Tony turned to him from the whiteboard, pen in hand and a look of mock horror on his face. "Quaint? Boss, you need to get out more. It's like the decorator was color blind and determined to make everything look like it was taken from a doll's house. Everything is so . . ." He shuddered as he sought the right word. "So frilly."

The detective gave the cadet a withering stare. "Okay, smart ass. I'm gonna call the chief."

Ryan picked up the receiver on the nearby rotary phone and dialed the precinct office. After a few moments, the chief picked up. The detective leaned back in his chair, collecting his thoughts. "Chief, it's me, Ryan."

The phone crackled. Perhaps it was the storm wreaking havoc on the phone lines. The chief's rasping voice sounded distant. "Ryan. Are you boys making any progress?"

Ryan considered the question for a moment. He knew that resolving this case was a priority for the chief. "Yeah, I think we are on to something."

"Look, the coroner called. Said he was able to identify some of the markings on the body, caused by pine needles puncturing the skin of the victim. They thought it was just environmental contamination from the Hudson, but they cross-checked the reports on the other homicide cases and they all had the same. The coroner said it was as though the bodies were . . ." He could hear the chief leafing through the coroner's report for the exact words. "Dragged through pine needles from . . . Wait a sec. From a Douglas fir tree."

Ryan considered the new information. The bodies were all connected by a Douglas fir pine tree. He scratched at the stubble on his chin. "That's a Christmas tree. No, wait! They're the same trees they grow up here on the local farm for the city."

There was a moment of silence as the chief weighed the detective's words. "Is that good? Anyway. I hope you get home tonight for the carols at the precinct. I don't need to remind you that the mayor will be here."

Ryan's mind was still distracted by the latest findings. They now had a clear connection between all of the victims: the Christmas trees grown here on Old Man Johnson's farm. "Yeah. We'll do our best, chief. We'll keep you updated."

He put down the receiver slowly, fearing he would break his mind's fragile focus on establishing a connection that this new piece of evidence could provide. He took a slow sip of his coffee and turned to the cadet. "Did you get that, Tony? Freakin' Christmas trees linking all the homicide cases."

Tony had seen Ryan like this before. His eyes had a slightly glazed look to them, like he was playing over some movie in the privacy of his mind that only he could see.

Tony nodded. "Yeah. Got it. What, you don't think they were killed by Christmas trees, do ya?" he asked in a sarcastic tone with a laugh.

The detective appeared to ignore him as he spoke more to himself in a hushed tone. "Christmas trees link all the crime scenes. Old Man Johnson's farm has a pine tree plantation that grows Douglas fir. I smell a connection here. Let's review the last few files that Cindy sent over. See if we can join all the dots here."

He appeared to break from his reverie and dropped a pile of papers on the desk next to Tony. "Here, you take that bundle. I'll take the rest."

CHAPTER 13
Joining the Dots

The scribbled web of connections on the whiteboard had grown substantially. They had drained several pots of coffee and were both feeling sharp and energized. Ryan leaned back in the chair and looked up approvingly at the board and Tony's handiwork.

The detective took a deep breath and steepled his fingers across his chest. Tony was wise enough to know that Ryan was about to test the cadet's reasoning and deduction abilities that represented the fundamental skills to solve any case. "So, cadet. Remember every crime has two elements. Number one: the *mens rea*."

The statement appeared to catch Tony off guard. "Men's what?"

Ryan shot him one of his reproachful looks. "Didn't you learn any Latin at school? *Mens rea*. The state of mind. The motivation. Find the motivation, and you find who committed the crime."

Tony relaxed slightly. "Sounds easy enough."

Ryan let his gaze linger on the quiet motel gardens behind the window. "And element number two:

the *actus reus*. The wrongful act itself. How was the crime perpetrated? What weapon was used? Is there a *modus operandi* here? A pattern of behavior? An obvious pattern often means that the killer is getting lazy. Cocky. And then there's the evidence that glues all this together and makes it stick to the killer. And in a court of law that's beyond reasonable doubt that our killer committed the murders. *Beyond reasonable doubt*, not one hundred per cent certainty. It's all about the weight of evidence." Ryan paused for a moment to let his words sink in. "So, what do we have here?"

Tony got up from the table and approached the whiteboard. His eyes searched the tangle of connections and facts that he had assembled. After a few seconds, he turned to Ryan. "I got something. Cindy's file included a report of the incident where Old Man Johnson got trampled by his own bull. And get this. Maybe it's a coincidence —"

"In police investigations, there are no coincidences," Ryan interjected, arching his eyebrows.

The cadet nodded and continued. "But it happened the week after Doctor Stewart took over Old Man Johnson's farm."

Ryan grunted in approval. "Good. I like it. The mysterious doctor who evaded our visit earlier and a plantation of Christmas trees seem to link the murders."

Tony continued, gathering momentum. "And the appearance of officials every year in town at the

Orchard Diner, meeting up with the good doctor."

Ryan nodded slowly and smiled. The cadet was upping his game. Tony might have the potential to make a great officer. "I think it's time we paid the doctor a little visit at the farm, don't you think?"

They were interrupted by a sudden knock on the door. Cindy appeared in her uniform with a big grin on her face, glancing around at their workspace. "Hey there, you guys. Hard at work, eh? I brought you some homemade cookies from Old Man Johnson's farm. They are just to die for!"

There it was again. *They are just to die for*. It was a strangely foreboding turn of phrase. Ryan had to think for a moment where he had heard it before. Then he remembered. Debbie, the waitress, had used the same words when she served them their pear pie at the diner earlier. He had just said so himself: there were no coincidences in murder inquiries. Ryan could feel himself being dragged by a wave to the inexorable conclusion to this case file. They just needed to join the dots here to make sense of all the clues they had gathered.

Cindy placed a packet of cookies on the table in front of the detectives.

Tony took a sip of his coffee and reached for the packet. He stopped, overcome by a sudden bout of coughing.

"You okay, Tony?" Ryan asked with concern.

Tony struggled to catch his breath. His words came in a harsh, whispered voice. "The cookies! Look at the packet."

Cindy gave Ryan a sideways look. "Is he okay?"

Ryan shrugged. "I dunno. I mean, he really likes chocolate chip cookies. Maybe he's just hungry—"

"Look! The victims. Wait," Tony said, as he managed to compose himself. He grabbed the case file and began flicking through the pages until he appeared to find what he was looking for. "Look, all the victims had a little arrow on their bodies. We were wrong. It wasn't an arrow, it's a Christmas tree!"

"Yeah, that's the trademark used for Old Man Johnson's farm," said Cindy in confusion.

The full realization of this suddenly dawned on Ryan as he grabbed the photos of one of the victims, comparing the triangular mark on their heads with the unassuming Christmas tree logo on the side of the package of cookies. There was no doubt. The killer had left his mark on each victim.

Ryan gave Tony a knowing look that said a thousand words. The kid was good.

The detective stood up and grabbed his jacket and hat. "Cindy, we need to get over to the farm right away!"

Cindy stopped them as they were about to leave the room. "Wait! If that's your car parked out front, you're gonna have to dig it out." Ryan shoulders sagged and he shook his head.

Cindy held up her hand. "Say, don't worry. I'll take you over in mine. It's got snow chains on it, a snowplow and all. Sheriff lets me borrow it sometimes."

Ryan brightened at the offer. "You are an angel, Cindy."

CHAPTER 14
Old Man Johnson's Farm

The snowplow left huge furrows in its wake, like a ship surging through pale water. They traversed a white wonderland beyond the village of Stone Ridge, the snow chains rattling and clunking heavily underneath them as they passed through deserted country roads. The scenery of orderly hedgerows and fields was all veiled in a white blanket of snow.

To the detective, every road they encountered looked the same, but Cindy drove the vehicle with purpose, meandering down one snow-covered roadway and then up another, bulldozing their way through heavy mounds of snow, which would have been impassable in a regular vehicle. Overhead dark angry storm clouds loomed ominously, and a low boom of thunder echoed across the landscape.

Cindy gave Ryan a broad grin. She was obviously enjoying herself immensely. "Awesome, huh?" She declared proudly. "We call it the beast. Three hundred brake horsepower. Don't worry. We'll get you to the farm."

"Yeah, I love it," he said returning a half-hearted

smile. He was getting a headache from the roar of the engine.

Cindy turned a sharp left, and they passed through a heavy wrought iron gate. A nearby large wooden sign half buried under snow read: Welcome to Old Man Johnson's Farm. Established 1864. Stone Ridge, New York.

They followed a roadway to a stand of conifers, their boughs laden with snow.

"Here we go. Just over there. There's the sign for the farm shop," Cindy said as she gestured to a low, flat building.

Ryan surveyed the area around them from the higher vantage point that the snowplow afforded. The snowfall had eased off for the first time in hours, which made it easier to get their bearings. The surrounding terrain was a brilliant white, and as the setting sun tried to peak through a passing cloud, Ryan was blinded momentarily. "You can let us out here," he said, shielding his eyes from the glare.

Cindy pulled the vehicle up near the trees and killed the ignition. In the silence that followed, Ryan's ears were ringing. Searching through the glove compartment, she recovered a large flashlight, which she handed to the detective. "There's a map of the farm on the information sign just over there. Oh, and you boys better take this. We're starting to lose the daylight."

Ryan turned to Tony in the back seat, signaling him they were ready to go. "Thanks Cindy. You're a star. You just sit tight."

Ryan jumped down from the snowplow, cursing softly as he landed in deep snow. How many pairs of socks did he need? Tony followed behind the detective, alert like a dog, long overdue his daily walk.

They made their way slowly, trudging through the banks of snow. Ryan paused at a glass paneled information board, rubbing off a layer of ice to get a better look at the map of the farm hidden underneath.

"So boss, what's the first stop?" Tony asked enthusiastically.

Ryan squinted through the glass, trying to get his bearings. His eyes searched for any features that would provide some clue as to the way they should proceed. "Let's get orientated in the farm shop. See if anyone's around."

They followed the path up a gentle slope to the farm shop. Christmas lights twinkled cheerily in the windows. Ryan pushed open the door of the shop slowly, and as it creaked open, the bell over the door gave a little welcoming tinkle. The detective cursed silently to himself. What the hell was the obsession with these damn bells? So much for any element of surprise. The whole farm would now know they were there.

Ryan entered the farm shop cautiously, checking all of the likely places that someone could be and then making a mental note of all the corners and doorways from which someone might emerge. It was burned into his mind to always look for the strategic advantage when entering a potentially dangerous crime scene. He paused and looked around him. The small shop had a counter with some freshly prepared food, a fridge, and a hot drinks area, and on the other side was a series of shelves, neatly arranged with farm produce. On the entrance side of the shop, there was a series of information panels telling the history of the farm over the years, displaying old photographs and farm-related paraphernalia. A second door on the back wall afforded the only other access.

"Hello. Anyone here?" the detective's voice broke the brooding silence.

Tony appeared in his peripheral vision, moving his way in the gloom along one of the aisles of farm products. He held up a packet of cookies with a big grin on his face. "Wow. Look at the size of these cookies," he announced approvingly in a hushed tone.

Ryan could feel a chill begin at the base of his back, growing steadily, like someone was immersing his spine in ice cold water. His guardian angel had alighted on his shoulder again. He could feel it, warning him to proceed with utmost care. He turned to the cadet, his voice a harsh urgent whisper. "Tony, focus now. Keep your eyes open. I can feel it. It's almost show time."

Tony registered the intense look in Ryan's eyes. A sudden noise drew his attention to the food counter. He gestured at the detective and said softly.

"Over there. There's someone over there behind the counter."

Ryan stepped in front of him with his hand raised. His other hand moved reflexively for the weight of his handgun holstered under his jacket. "Okay, take my lead."

There was an unearthly screech and clatter of fallen plates as a large cat raced through Ryan's legs and disappeared from view. Ryan could feel his heart hammering loudly in his ears. He felt as though he had just aged a few years.

Tony's face was pale and drawn. "Jesus! That cat scared the . . . Ouch!"

Ryan clipped him on the back of the head and gave him one of his "I told you not to do that" kind of looks.

Tony nodded, distracted by something in the exhibition area near the window. "Is that a painting of Old Man Johnson?" he asked, studying the display.

Ryan joined him for a better look at the painting. They stood side by side for a few moments in the empty farm shop, critically examining the oil painting. It was dark and the surface cracked with age. It depicted a young man holding a long pitchfork, standing next to an old stone wall.

"Yeah. Looks like it," said Ryan. "When he was younger, I guess. Creepy looking fellow."

The detective's eyes searched the exhibition of information panels on the wall for anything else of interest and his gaze was drawn to a series of black and white photos of cattle. Underneath were several rosettes declaring first prize. "Look at the size of those bulls. They're like monsters." Some of the cattle were grossly oversized, or maybe it was just the angle of the photographer.

Tony tapped his finger on another map of the farm. "Here's a map of the farm again. We're just on the western side of the farm, nearest to the main road. Looks like it's a short walk through the fields to the outbuildings. Here, look. That's where they grow the Christmas trees." He gave Ryan a thoughtful look. "Did you get your Christmas tree yet, boss?"

Since they had entered the shop, the shadows around them had lengthened. It was getting difficult to read the map now. Ryan peered out the window. All that was left of the day was an orange glow in the sky, like the land beyond the western horizon was burning. The detective pushed the disturbing thought from his mind. He was acutely aware that they were running out of time for their investigation. They needed to move quickly now, or they would end up searching the farm in complete darkness. He held onto a shred of hope that they could still make it home to the city to celebrate Christmas Eve with their families.

"Okay, let's . . . shh! What's that sound?" Ryan asked urgently, putting a hand on Tony's shoulder in warning. He could hear a distant buzzing sound, like a giant angry wasp.

The whining grew in intensity and then drifted away from them.

"It's a snowmobile," said Tony. "Heading away

from here."

CHAPTER 15

Into the Abyss

From inside the farm shop, Ryan stared out across the fields stretching away from the main access road. Through the dimness, he could make out a dark shadow speeding up a snowy incline, leaving a long trench behind it. "There it is," the detective said. "It's gone off east into the farm. Let's follow it." He turned to the cadet, his eyes meeting Tony's and holding his gaze monetarily with a determined look. "Keep your firearm ready," he instructed softly.

Ryan led the way through the rear door of the store into what appeared to be some kind of maintenance yard for the farm. Various items of machinery were strewn about, half buried under snow. The snow had stopped completely now, replaced by a leaden silence that seemed to drape itself around them. As they walked across the yard, the crunching sound of their footsteps was almost deafening. Tony stopped Ryan with his arm. "Hey, boss," he said, pointing across to the nearby field. "There are more snowmobiles parked over there."

The detective followed Tony's gaze and his eyes lingered on the sleek form of two snowmobiles, like two dark sharks beached on the snow. A barely perceptible chill tingled through Ryan's being. Every instinct he had honed over the last twenty years of his police work and investigation warned him to be careful. But Tony was already striding forward through the snow, reminding him of a kid racing to the candy shop, oblivious to everything but the reward in sight.

Ryan grabbed the cadet strongly by the shoulder, almost tripping him up. "Wait! That would be too easy," His breath came in plumes of vapor from his mouth. There was a lingering scent, oddly out at place with the chill freshness of the country air.

"What's that smell?" the detective asked, his nose wrinkling with distaste. And then he realized what it was. Diesel. Someone had rigged the fuel tanks of the snowmobiles to explode. "Move!" he yelled, pushing the cadet roughly away from the snowmobiles and into a deep snowdrift.

Just as they both hit the ground, the air was rent by an ear-splitting explosion. Lumps of metal whined past them, and the farm shop windows shattered.

Tony emerged from the snow beside Ryan, blinking in alarm as his ears recovered from the boom of the blast. "Good spot, boss!'" he gasped. "Guess that means someone doesn't want us here."

The detective considered the cadet's words. They were now in what police referred to as "hot pursuit."

They were just minutes behind someone who had deliberately tried to impede their investigation, if not kill them. The whole day had led them to this place, this very moment. This is where the trail would end, for them or for the killer. Hot pursuit was the license they needed to justify them following the suspect wherever he ran. There could be no escape.

"Yeah, guess so," Ryan answered, breathing hard. "But as my wife always says, I can be like a dog with a bone and I ain't letting this one go." He stood slowly to his feet, helping up the cadet and brushed the snow off his jacket. "Come on. Let's follow the tracks."

Whoever the person on the snowmobile was, their actions had become desperate. They had banked on stopping the officers by blowing up the other two snowmobiles and had left a trail behind them that was effectively a great signpost as to where they had gone. There was no longer any need to search for breadcrumbs.

"Trail leads into the pines," said Tony as he surveyed the monochromatic landscape. *The pines*, thought the detective to himself. All the victims in the cases files were connected by pine trees somehow. All connected to this farm. How did a Christmas tree link them all?

They made their way slowly across the open fields, dragging themselves through the drifts of snow. The storm had abated, and the remaining wind seemed only to touch the highest branches of the towering pine trees. It sounded like the breathing of a gigantic animal that was slumbering restlessly. The detective had the disturbing impression that the entire world around them was drawing its last breath for the final act.

The silence was broken by a spluttering sound of machinery coming from the forest of pine trees. "What the hell is that noise?" asked Ryan.

They listened for a moment, pausing at the edge of the pine plantation, not daring to go any further. The snowmobile tracks had disappeared into the shadows of the trees.

"Sounds like heavy machinery," answered Tony in a hushed voice.

Ryan felt his jacket for the reassuring weight of his revolver concealed in its holster. Whoever they were pursuing knew they were coming and had likely prepared a welcome for them.

Ryan led the way into the gloom under the pine trees. Sharp branches snagged at his jacket, scratching his face as he pushed purposefully forward. Underfoot, gnarled roots tried their best to trip them. It was one of those places where he would hate to be ambushed. Anyone familiar with the terrain would have a massive advantage over them. They were blindly following a trail that they hoped would lead them to their goal, some resolution to this case file that had plagued the department for seven years now.

The trail ended in a wide clearing in the pines. Ryan stopped to take in their surroundings. It was twilight now, that curious mix of light and dark where the shadows lengthen and the day draws to a close. It was more difficult to discern the outlines of shapes in the gloom. A killer could be hiding anywhere. The clattering sound had grown louder and was almost deafening as they stood together in the clearing. In front of them was some type of a conveyor belt, happily grinding along. To one side was a pile of pine trees that had recently been chopped down. They were heaped in a great pile, like a funeral pyre of bodies, ready to be burned. *No*, Ryan thought. *Not burned. They were ready to be loaded on this machine and prepared for sale in the city.*

"So, this is the Christmas tree plantation," said Ryan appraising the scene critically. His eyes followed the line of machinery, evaluating how it worked. "The trees get loaded onto this belt. Go through this machine and get netted up with twine, so they're nice and easy for loading. Here, grab one of those trees there, will you? I wanna see how this thing works."

Tony grunted as he tugged one of the trees from the pile and heaved it onto the conveyor belt.

The detective watched the passage of the tree carefully, as the longest branches were trimmed and it was netted up, then stamped, and prepared for sale. All compact and ready for handling to be shipped downriver on the Hudson, bound for the city.

Ryan's mind was buzzing like a hive of bees, assessing the surroundings and comparing it in his mind to the case file, he had read dozens of times before. He could see the haunting black-and-white photographs of the victims. Their sightless eyes had been the cause of many restless nights for him, as though they had been pleading with him to find the truth. The detective began talking softly, almost to himself, repeating himself so that his brain was forced to review all of the facts before him. "So, the tree goes through, gets stamped and netted for sale." Without warning, the truth trampled him, like one of Old Man Johnson's prized bulls, stampeding through his tired mind and bringing with it the blinding truth.

"Jesus," exclaimed Ryan in a whisper, inspecting the base of the tree stump where the stamp had made its mark. "Look at the stamp! A little Christmas tree. It's the same mark that was on every victim's body. This is the murder weapon! The netting on the victims wasn't fishing net. It was netting from this machine!"

Time seemed to slow as the full realization hit them like a tsunami. All of the images in the files now made sense. Ryan recalled the words of the coroner that were related to him by the chief during their last call. All of the victims had puncture marks on their bodies, *as though they were dragged through pine trees*. They had been hauled into the pine forest to this makeshift abattoir. Ryan could almost hear their screams of protest, lost amid the moaning of the wind high in the treetops. He could see the victims in his mind, sadly acknowledging that this was how each of them met their untimely end. This is where their lives had been snuffed out, like the candles in the church that Ryan attended at the end of every mass.

Ryan's thoughts were broken by the angry whine of a snowmobile. It was coming closer.

He grabbed Tony and propelled him into action. "Tony, circle back into the trees! Stay out of view and stay sharp."

Tony didn't need to be told twice. He disappeared into the dark shadows of the pine trees.

Ryan braced himself for what was to come. His eyes searched the tree line for the killer. It seemed a fitting place to stage the final showdown. Here, in this monochrome world of dark trees and snow. The overbearing scent of pines hung in the air. There was a curious, almost magical glow to the snow as the sky darkened. The luminescence gave the scene a serene, ethereal quality about it, as though it was no longer reality. The detectives had trespassed into a dream world of the killer's own design and making.

"Stop and stay where you are. Put your hands up wide!" The voice had an educated ring to it but was as cold and emotionless as a snake. There was a moment of silence as a shadow emerged from the trees and stepped onto the glowing white snow. The stranger seemed to be taking the measure of the detective, sizing him up to determine whether he was a threat or just a mere annoyance.

"Who the hell are you?" he demanded, as he drew closer to Ryan.

Ryan could feel his blood turn to ice in his veins. He had met many killers over the years, and in his experience, the most dangerous ones were not the ones who were angry and enraged, but the ones who were calm and calculating. The latter usually had a very nasty habit of squirming free to continue their killing spree, as though somehow vindicated in their belief that they were superhuman and untouchable.

"NYPD," Ryan managed in a hoarse voice, as the stranger drew closer. He had to let the man know who he was dealing with, that he had finally been snared.

"My, oh, my. What have I done to deserve this honor? Detective, is it?" The man was now close enough now for Ryan to see him properly in the aura from the snow. He wore a parka with a thick fur-lined collar. His face was that of an academic, and he seemed out of place outside among the trees. His dark beady eyes studied Ryan behind round spectacles. He was small in stature, and if not for the curious metallic weapon that glinted threateningly in his arms, Ryan would have tried to overpower him. The detective decided to pursue a different tactic. He would buy himself time and keep his eyes alert for any weakness he could use.

"Detective Ryan," he confirmed, before pausing, taking a few seconds to calm himself, so that he could keep talking. "And well, maybe you can tell me what you've done." Ryan gestured at the long glinting object in the man's arms. "Put that down . . ." Ryan swallowed hard. "Is that a weapon you're pointing at me?"

The man stopped several feet from the detective, contemplating his next move. "Detective Ryan." He said the name as though the detective's name itself was bitter in his mouth. His lips broke into a cold sneer, giving his face a devilish character in the growing darkness. "Yes, this is a gun of sorts, at least. It's my own invention actually. I'm quite proud of it. It's a modified tranquilizer dart gun." He held it up, so that Ryan could see it clearly. "Meant for bulls," he said in a matter-of-fact tone of voice. "Calms them down. For you, the dosage in this would be quite lethal though." He let his words linger in the air. Ryan sensed that the stranger was enjoying himself now that he had the detective caught like a fly in his net.

Ryan could feel the adrenaline well inside him. His body was preparing for fight or flight. He glanced furtively around the dark clearing. There was nowhere to run, and if he tried to fight, the stranger would gun him down with his damn dart gun. He forced himself to take a deep steadying breath. He was not beaten yet, he told himself. He had been in worse situations. Hadn't he? His brain seemed unwilling to play along with this charade. He was walking on very thin ice now. One false step, and he would join the photos of all the victims. Just another number in a file for the next officer to investigate.

"If I don't report back to the precinct in the next

hour, this place will be crawling with officers," Ryan said abruptly. He would try intimidation. It was partly true, although what would his colleagues find really? There was a momentary lull in the storm, but if its full fury returned, it could be weeks before his body was recovered under the snow and ice.

The detective's words appeared to have the desired effect and gave the man pause for thought. He could see the stranger's rodent-like eyes glinting in the dark clearing as he surveyed the Christmas tree conveyor belt. "Hmm. I see you have acquainted yourself with my little Christmas helper here. So, you know too much already, I'm guessing." His eyes met the detective's. "I don't think I can let you go, Detective Ryan." A disturbing smile played about his lips. "Unless, of course, you promise to keep quiet." His eyes bore into the detective as he waited eagerly for his answer.

Ryan could see where this was going. The man was embarking on some delusion that would provide a twisted justification for killing him. That he would, according to his own skewed moral compass, be vindicated in getting rid of the detective.

Ryan's mind struggled to find an answer that would buy him more time. But before his thoughts could intervene, he blurted out. "I can't do that." His words sounded hollow and meaningless in the gathering blackness. Ryan had a growing feeling that he had intruded and did not belong in this cursed place, hidden from view by the towering pine trees.

"No. And I suppose you have worked out who I am?"

The question took Ryan by surprise. His mind was keenly focused on survival by any means, not some guessing game. But deep down, his detective brain had been whirring away in the background the whole time, and he knew well who the killer was. "You're the farm veterinarian, Doctor Stewart."

"Smart cookie, aren't you? My friends call me Stewie." He gave the detective an oddly vacant look that chilled Ryan's heart. "Are you my friend, Detective Ryan?" The rhetorical question hung in the darkness. "Kind of far from home, aren't you?" he asked casually.

Ryan could see that the doctor was now trying to paint him as the enemy, which would lead him to the inescapable conclusion that Ryan had to be eradicated. Frustration welled within Ryan. He had come so far, here to this lightless place in the middle of nowhere, only to fail at the very end.

"Yeah," the detective spat. "You could say that. I hate the countryside. It smells like cow shit everywhere!"

This seemed to genuinely amuse the doctor, and he let loose a dry laugh before collecting himself again. "You're funny. I like that. In another life, we could have been friends."

Ryan saw his opening. "You wanna hear something else that's funny? I think you killed all those people with that damn machine! Stamped them and netted them up. Then sent them down the Hudson River on one of your barges, packed up like damn Christmas trees, and threw their bodies in the water." He paused to let the full force of his accusation hit the veterinarian. "The one thing I just don't get is why."

Ryan felt that the man had taken the bait. It was irresistible for the killer to provide a perverse justification as to why he had carried out all the crimes. Ryan could see him gather his thoughts for his final revelation.

The doctor managed a muffled clap with his gloved hands as he cradled his tranquilizer gun. He nodded as though he had a newly found respect for the detective. "Now I know why they call you boys 'New York's finest.' But you, Ryan. You will be my last dance. My finest piece. And, really, can't you work out why?"

Ryan's investigative mind was still sifting through all the useless detritus to leave only the gleaming strands of truth. "You . . ." he began as he caught up with the recently hatched thoughts, fluttering wildly in his mind. "You tried to kill Old Man Johnson when he took over the farm!"

Dr. Stewart shook his head disapprovingly. "Please, the old man was half dead already. It was well meant. I mean, look at him now. I just left the gate open. The bull did the rest."

Ryan sought the motivation behind all of this. He tried for the usual one. "Was it money?" he asked.

The doctor sighed as though he was disappointed

with the detective. "It was at first. Do you know how much a prized herd of cattle is worth? Well, let's just say, it's a lot." He chuckled softly to himself. "I can't believe no one asked themselves why these cows are so damn big. So many prizes, year after year." He was overcome by a sudden fit of silent laughter. "Well, do I have to spell it out for you, Detective Ryan? It's not magic, you know. It's a banned growth hormone. The more of the game I played, the more complicated it became. Some unfortunate people came sniffing around here, thinking they were smart. They were smarter than most, I suppose. They figured out this little operation. And, as they say, the rest is history." He glanced up at the detective again, a faint smile on his thin lips. "I suppose you have a tidy file in your office on each of them."

The faces of all the victims appeared in Ryan's mind, as though they had been dredged from the murky depths of the Hudson. Their untimely demise had left behind them a terrible path of destruction. Their families, their friends. All scarred irrevocably beyond measure by their passing. He could feel the set of rosary beads in his pocket against his skin. They somehow offered more comfort than his heavy holstered handgun in the presence of this monster. "You killed all those people. Just to protect this farm?" he asked in disbelief.

The doctor shook his head. "No detective," he answered. "Not just this farm. This whole town.

Without this farm, Stone Ridge wouldn't exist. It would just be another green meadow in the Catskills."

He stopped abruptly, nodding solemnly. Ryan could sense that he had run out of words. This was the end of the doctor's sermon, and this final confession was as much as he was prepared to share with the detective. He arched his back and eased his neck from side to side. It gave the detective the impression of a snake that was preparing to strike, limbering up for the final fatal attack.

"Sorry, I am getting bored of this conversation. I don't have a very long attention span," the doctor said, readying the tranquilizer gun in his arm. Clicking off the safety mechanism, he raised the barrel to point directly at the detective's chest. He was at point-blank range. This was it. In all his worst nightmares, he never envisaged dying like this. Ryan's hand searched again for the rosary beads in his pocket. He grabbed them, like a drowning man desperate to keep himself afloat in dark waters.

"You won't get away with killing me . . ." he managed, but his words rang hollow, without any sense of conviction.

The doctor's eyes were two deep pools of blackness as he looked at him, sizing him up for slaughter, while his finger caressed the trigger. "In this snowstorm? Really? Communications are down. Your body will float down the Hudson tonight and end up in New York sometime in the New Year." He raised the gun directly at the detective's heart.

Ryan could feel himself go cold, as though someone had poured freezing water into the chambers of his heart. "You piece of shit!" He screamed loudly.

The doctor smirked again. "Your arms will pop out of joint," he laughed manically and then managed to control his mirth. "It's actually quite funny to watch really."

The seconds slowed to a crawl in the gathering gloom. *Tick-tock. Tick-tock.*

Ryan looked down the thin barrel of the weapon, waiting for the pain that it would unleash upon him. And he had expected this to be just another field trip. Another investigation that would end up resolved and the chief would be happy. He saw the doctor's trigger finger move a millimeter. He braced himself for the inevitable pain. How did he end up here in some backwater? Would his passing really be marked by just a number in a dusty file? His family would be torn apart and probably never learn what happened to him.

He could feel his heart beating loudly in his ears. The sound of the gunshot cut the silence like a knife. A flock of birds took flight from the shadows of the trees. He realized in horror that he had not taken another breath. It was as though someone had turned off his functions. He fell slowly to his knees onto the snow. There was a sharp rushing sound as he gasped again, and cool night air came flooding into his lungs again. He could still breathe!

The detective saw the doctor drop his weapon and clutch at his chest. He stared at the detective in confusion as his hand came away from his jacket, dark with blood. He staggered for a moment and then fell heavily to the ground, like a marionette whose strings had been cut.

Ryan saw a silhouetted figure emerge from the trees, a gun held low in its outstretched hand. And then the detective understood what had happened. It was Tony. The cadet walked slowly as if he was in a trance.

The detective got to his feet unsteadily. "Tony!" he yelled hoarsely. "Jesus, I thought I was . . ." He ran to the cadet; the revolver the young officer was carrying still smoked in the night air. Tony had a look of serene disbelief on his face. "Don't freeze. Don't freeze." His tearful eyes met Ryan's and the detective could see the fear and pain etched in the cadet's face. "No, boss," the cadet managed. "That was me. Assess. Evaluate the Risk. Pull the trigger. I . . ."

Tony dropped his handgun in the snow and started sobbing uncontrollably. Ryan reached for him and hugged the kid close. "Jesus, I pulled the trigger, boss!" he wailed into the detective's shoulder.

Ryan held him for a moment, letting him get it all out. Tony was overcome by shock, his entire body trembled in Ryan's arms. It was the first time he had been forced to pull a gun on someone. Whatever happened, he would never be the same. Taking the life of another human being, even a monster like Dr. Stewart, took its toll on a person's soul. The cadet would forever bear that mark. He would need Ryan's help to come to terms with his decision.

"Tony. It's okay. You did the right thing. Hey, you did the right thing. Look at me." Tony looked up and saw the tears streaming down Ryan's face. The detective held him by both arms and gave him a silent nod of understanding. The cadet managed a feeble smile in return.

They stood there for a moment in the darkness comforting each other, as the wind howled its mournful song in the treetops, and snowflakes began to fall slowly again from the brooding sky.

CHAPTER 16

Carols at the Precinct

Ryan had never been so glad to return to the city. Manhattan welcomed them with open arms, embracing them in its warm glow of streetlamps and hubbub of traffic. After the detective had called in the local sheriff to secure the crime scene, he had left the hamlet of Stone Ridge behind with all of its secrets. He would not be sad if he never returned there. He made a silent vow that he would never complain about the city again. This is where he belonged, amid the warren of crowded avenues and streets.

Cindy, the sheriff's liaison officer, had let the officers borrow the snowplow for the return trip to the city, and they had made good progress through the devastation that the snowstorm had left in its wake. The trip had taken them a few hours, but Ryan couldn't argue with that. At least they were back home, just in time for Christmas Eve. He had a pounding headache from the relentless growl of the engine and his back ached. Ryan had let the cadet drive back to keep his mind off what had happened under the dark pine trees of Stone Ridge.

Ryan surveyed the street in front of the precinct office and spied a space large enough to accommodate the cumbersome vehicle. "Well, let's just park this thing. Over there. Who cares? It's not like we're going to get a parking ticket, is it?"

The cadet killed the ignition, and Ryan sighed in relief. "God, I think I've gone deaf after that ride home."

Tony exhaled deeply and his shoulders sagged with exhaustion. He turned to Ryan. "Well, at least we made it back. It was nice of Cindy to loan us her ride, boss."

Ryan yawned. "Yeah, it was. Put her on our Christmas card list."

Tony closed his eyes, overcome with fatigue. "I sure am tired, boss."

Ryan nodded. Saying it had been a long day, was a profound understatement. He felt as though they had compressed a whole year into just one single day. Every part of him ached. "I know. Me too. Let's go in and pack our stuff. Sing those carols to make the chief happy and get home to our families for Christmas Eve." A thought struck him suddenly. Christmas. He didn't have any gift for his wife. He had managed to get a present for their daughter weeks ago that was stashed away in Ryan's special hiding place he used for all occasions, including Christmas and birthdays.

"Oh, no! I still don't have anything for my wife. She's gonna kill me!" Ryan declared in dismay.

Tony brightened up. "Don't worry, boss. Cindy left you some goodies from Old Man Johnson's farm. You know, to say thanks for all our support with this case. She left me a pack of extra-large chocolate cookies." The cadet reached into the back seat and produced a brightly colored bag, emblazoned with little festive Christmas trees. "Here."

Ryan rummaged through the contents of the bag and grunted with satisfaction. "Hmm. Some handmade chocolates and cookies from Old Man Johnson's farm. Better than nothing, I guess. And what's this?" he asked with a smirk, pulling out a cuddly animal toy. "It's one of those hand-sewn cows. Here, there's two of them. Happy Christmas, Tony," the detective said handing it the cadet. "You earned it."

Tony looked at it suspiciously. As he took hold of it, the cow made an unsettling mechanical mooing sound. "Er, thanks, boss."

Ryan paused for a moment before he got out of the car. "Oh, hey Tony. Listen. Let's forget about that little episode earlier, okay? You did good back there."

Tony swallowed nervously and nodded silently.

They entered the precinct office in a flurry of snowflakes and cold air. The whole NYPD precinct team was standing around the chief, who was sitting on one of the desks in the center of the room. He gave them a conspiratorial wink. He had obviously been expecting their return. Christmas garlands and twinkling lights adorned every corner of the office.

The chief grinned broadly as the detective and cadet entered the room. "Well," the chief began. "If it isn't my favorite dynamic duo."

The office broke into cheers and clapping. The news had clearly reached the precinct of their successful resolution of the Christmas Eve murders case file. The chief silenced the clapping with a raise of his hand. "Ryan, you have my thanks and the mayor's for resolving this case. I've been on the phone to the sheriff's office up in Stone Ridge. The whole of Old Man Johnson's farm has been declared a crime scene. Forensics are taking the place apart. Preliminary findings have already established sufficient evidence of the homicides. This is the county sheriff's case now, since all the killings happened in Ulster County. So, we wash our hands of the Christmas Eve murders file, and you continue your perfect record of resolving every damn case we give you!"

The office broke into applause again. The chief held up his huge hand for quiet. "And so it is my real pleasure to award you the rank of first grade detective! Happy Christmas, Detective Ryan, first grade."

The chief was unable to control the uproar that followed. He yelled over the noise "Now get the hell out of here, all of you, and sing like your lives depended on it! The mayor is waiting for the NYPD's carol evening!"

They dispersed out into the courtyard area of the precinct office and filed along the steps, where a large crowd had gathered excitedly on the sidewalk. Ryan caught a glimpse of Father Murphy standing next to the mayor, wrapped in a scarf and woolen hat against the biting cold. Snowflakes fell gently from the sky. And they really sang like their lives depended on it. Although Ryan was exhausted, he was overcome by a joy of just being alive. He glanced over at Tony as they sang to the music of the brass band and gave the cadet a broad smile. Sure, Tony could be a pain in the ass sometimes, but damn was he happy the kid could shoot like that. Their little day trip upstate had been a revelation for Ryan. He was now pretty certain that Tony had the potential to be a great detective, perhaps with a guiding hand from Ryan, even good enough to join the exalted ranks of New York's finest.

ABOUT THE AUTHOR

David J. Kinsella originally hails from the fair city of Dublin, Ireland, and currently lives with his family in London, United Kingdom.

Printed in Great Britain
by Amazon